"How could they

Aaron ran a hand through his tangle of dark hair. "How could a creature of Heaven be so cruel?"

"Verchiel and his followers have not been creatures of Heaven for quite some time," Belphegor replied. "They lost sight of that special place a long time ago."

"Why can't he just leave me alone?" Aaron asked, the weight of his responsibilities beginning to wear upon him. "Why does it have to be this way?"

Belphegor sighed as he looked up at the early morning sky above Aerie. "Verchiel's still fighting the war, I think," he said after a bit of thought. "So caught up in righting a wrong, that he can't accept the idea that the battle is over. There's a new age dawning, Aaron." Belphegor slowly squatted down, and Aaron could hear the popping of his ancient joints. "Whether he likes it or not."

Aaron looked into the old angel's eyes, searching for a bit of strength he could borrow.

"And you're the harbinger," he continued. "Whether *you* like it or not."

Marshall County Public Library
1003 Poplar Street
Benton, KY 42025

Read all of **the fallen** titles:

the fallen

Book Three

aerie

Thomas E. Sniegoski

Simon Pulse

NEW YORK   LONDON   TORONTO   SYDNEY   SINGAPORE

If you purchased this book without a cover, you should be aware that this book is stolen property. It was reported as "unsold and destroyed" to the publisher, and neither the author nor the publisher has received any payment for this "stripped book."

This book is a work of fiction. Any references to historical events, real people, or real locales are used fictitiously. Other names, characters, places, and incidents are the product of the author's imagination, and any resemblance to actual events or locales or persons, living or dead, is entirely coincidental.

First Simon Pulse edition November 2003

Copyright © 2003 by Thomas E. Sniegoski

SIMON PULSE
An imprint of Simon & Schuster
Children's Publishing Division
1230 Avenue of the Americas
New York, NY 10020

All rights reserved, including the right of reproduction in whole or in part in any form.

Designed by Sammy Yuen Jr.
The text of this book was set in 11 point Palatino.

Printed in the United States of America
4 6 8 10 9 7 5 3

Library of Congress Control Number 2003105392

ISBN 0-689-85307-6

For Launey Fogg. His words of encouragement will be treasured forever, as will his memory.

Thank you, as always, to my loving and oh-so-patient wife, LeeAnne, and my four-legged pally, Mulder.

Lots of special thanks with sprinkles to my brother, separated at birth, Christopher Golden, and to the Termineditor with a vengeance, Lisa Clancy, and her assistant to the stars, Lisa Gribbin.

And special thanks minus the sprinkles must go to: Mom and Dad, Eric Powell, Dave Kraus, David Carroll, Doctor Kris, Tom and Lori Stanley, Paul Griffin, Tim Cole, and the usual suspects, Jon and Flo, Bob and Pat, Don Kramer, Pete Donaldson, Ken Curtis, and Zach Howard. And remember folks, be good to your parents; they've been good to you.

aerie

prologue

It never seems to rest, Alastor reflected as he shoveled the last bit of a hearty breakfast of eggs, bacon, and toast into his yawning maw. He belched powerfully, speckling his ample front with flecks of chewed food, and dropped the greasy paper plate to the floor beside his leather recliner. It was nine o'clock in the morning, and what the fallen angel had hidden in the basement of the Bourbonnais, Illinois, home was already calling out to him.

"Alastor," it whispered like the buzzing of a housefly. *"Come, Alastor. Look upon what you have cast away."*

Alastor chose to ignore it. *The monkeys, Reggie and Katie,* he thought as his eyes caught the clock on the wall, *they're often amusing.* He snatched up the remote control in a meaty hand, scattering potato chip bags and candy bar wrappers from atop the coffee table before him. He would lose himself in the trifle of morning television, a distraction from the incessant whispers in the cellar.

"Do you remember what it was like before the war—before you listened to the seductive reasonings of the Morningstar? Do you remember, Alastor?"

"Quiet!" the angel spat. He jabbed a sausage-thick finger down onto the remote to turn up the volume, settling his excessive bulk back into the recliner. It was a cooking segment, which he enjoyed, as mouthwatering meals were prepared by world-renowned chefs with the assistance of the program's hosts.

Reggie dropped an egg on the floor and the studio audience went wild with laughter. Alastor joined in the hilarity, captivated by the antics of the human monkeys. If the Creator had ever bothered to mention how thoroughly entertaining these fragile creatures could be, he would never have pledged allegiance to the Son of the Morning.

"Remember what you once were, Alastor of the heavenly host Virtues. Come and recall your former glory."

The audience was laughing again and Alastor seethed. He had missed the latest morsel of primitive humor.

"Damn you, be quiet!" he screamed, driving a fleshy fist down onto the chair's worn armrest. "I looked at you yesterday—and the day before that. I have no desire to see you now."

The chef produced a soufflé from the oven

and the audience showed their approval with a burst of applause. Feigning exuberance, Katie explained how to acquire the recipe for the delectable dish, and he thought about writing the information down, but the whispers from the cellar beckoned for his attention.

"A chance to remember how you once were—the beauty and the power . . ."

Alastor hauled his bulky mass up out of the chair, a rain of crumbs from his last meal sprinkling down to the refuse-strewn floor. "I am still beautiful and still powerful," he bellowed, one eye fixed on the morning program, lest he miss something of importance. The *Reggie and Katie* show broke to a commercial about adult diapers and the angel turned his full attention to the taunting voice.

"What will it take to shut you up?" he growled, knowing full well what the answer would be, what the answer always was.

"Look at me," the whispers hissed. *"Look at me and remember our time together."*

Alastor turned back to the television. A dog food commercial was showing—a small human child playing with puppies.

"No matter how often I see you, it never satisfies your need," the fallen angel grumbled, wondering offhandedly how the dog food would taste.

"And it never shall. I will not allow you to forget what we once were."

"Even if that is what *I* desire?" he asked, his attention drawn to an ad for the talk show that would follow *Reggie and Katie*. The show's topic would be crib death, and he smiled with the secret knowledge of things that the simple human brain could barely begin to perceive. If he were so inclined, he could tell them all why their babies die in the night. If he were so inclined.

"I have no interest in your desire," said the voice from the basement. *"Come and look upon me or I shall taunt you all the rest of the day and well into the night."*

Reggie and Katie returned, and it took all the strength that Alastor could muster to pull his eyes from the entertaining visuals. "If I spend time with you now, you'll not bother me for the remainder of this day?" he asked, shambling closer to the kitchen.

"Yes, come and look."

Alastor lurched into the kitchen, gasping for breath as he propelled himself toward the cellar door, eager for the promise of blissful silence.

"Anything for some peace," he growled, in his mind planning his television viewing for the remainder of the day.

His sweatpants began to slip below his middle, and he reached down to pull the elastic waistband up over his protruding stomach.

"Peace. An unattainable pursuit since our fall from Heaven; do you ever think we'll experience its bliss again?" the bothersome voice asked through

the door as Alastor took hold of the knob and turned it, a cool dampness wafting up from below as he pulled the cellar door open.

"I've found my own peace," he said irritably, leaning on the rail to carefully descend the wooden steps that creaked in protest beneath his weight. "Is it what I knew in Heaven? No, but I will never see the likes of that again."

He stood at the bottom of the stairs and glanced around, surveying his accumulation of goods, items he had acquired in the years since deciding he would live as a human. There was furniture, enough to fill multiple dwellings; boxes of books, clothes, and kitchen implements; tools; cans of paint; three lawnmowers; at least four televisions still in their boxes; and so much more stored away out of sight.

Alastor remembered when he had made the choice. The Powers were on the hunt, and he knew that it was only a matter of time before they found him. It was all about survival, so he did the unthinkable.

"That was your second fall," the creeping voice spoke from within the room, pulling him from the past. *"When you attempted to sever our bond."*

Alastor lurched forward toward the source of his irritation, his slippered feet scuffling across the cool, concrete floor. Carefully he maneuvered around an ancient bureau. "There was no other way," he said, almost losing his balance as he stepped over a wooden milk crate filled with old toys made from tin. "It was that, or die." The fallen angel steadied himself with the help of a foldaway bed, and continued on toward the object of his torment. "I had no choice," he said again, perhaps more to convince himself. "How many times must I tell you?"

Everything that had defined him had been lost during the war. Alastor had fled to Earth with others of his ilk, the fearsome Powers in pursuit. For countless centuries he wandered the planet, purposeless, hiding from his would-be punishers. He had almost decided to give up and accept his fate, when it came to him: He would hide amongst the natives. He would become one of them, renouncing everything that defined him as a being of Heaven.

It was a perfect plan. By giving up his angel's ways and surrounding himself with all things human, Alastor hoped to mask his scent from the Powers that hunted him. The angel glanced across the basement, catching his reflection in a mirror against the wall.

"*Look at you*," the voice said from close by, dripping with disdain. "*Look at what has become of you.*"

Alastor was fat, morbidly so, but that was all part of the mask he wore. "I've explained why I must be this way," the angel said, eyes fixed upon the mirror.

For millienia the angel had found the concept of humanity revolting and then had been shocked at how easy it was to be one of them—how simply he slipped into the role of humanity—and he found the experience to be quite enjoyable most of the time. Alastor had grown particularly fond of eating and television.

The fallen angel looked away from the mirror, suddenly unnerved by his grotesque appearance. "I tell you there was no other way." He continued through the basement, drawing closer to the source of his tribulation.

"I'm here," he announced, his breath coming in wheezing gasps as he stopped before a large wooden table bolted to the wall. The top of the workplace had been cleared away, the only uncluttered surface in the entire room, and resting on it was a long, cardboard box.

"*Do you miss us?*" asked the voice in a sibilant whisper that tickled his ears.

Alastor felt the scars on his back begin to burn and itch beneath his heavy, cotton sweatshirt—slightly at first, but growing to the point where he wished he could tear the flesh from his back to make it stop. He gripped the ends of the table and squeezed.

"Of course I miss you, but . . ."

"*Take us back,*" the voice commanded, hissing. "*Make us whole again. It was never supposed to be this way.*"

The fallen angel shook his head sadly, the flesh of his face and neck wobbling with his repressed emotion. "If I were to do that, I would most certainly be destroyed," he said, fighting back tears.

He reached for the box flaps that hid the artifacts of his past and pried them apart, the scars upon his shoulder blades screaming for his attention.

"But we would be together again," the whisper from within the box cajoled. *"As we are meant to be."*

Alastor had wrapped them in sheets of plastic to protect them from the dampness. He gasped as he always did when he looked upon them, never fully remembering the extent of his sacrifice. He started to close up the box, not wanting to be reminded.

"Look at me," the voice within the box demanded.

"I have looked," he responded slowly. "And as usual, I am filled with an overwhelming sadness."

"Unwrap us," it ordered. *"Look upon us and remember."*

Alastor found himself doing as the voice requested, pulling back the plastic wrap to expose the box's contents. He remembered the pain—the decision, as well as the act itself—to sever from his body the final remnant of what separated him from the monkeys.

To be human, they had to be cut off.

Alastor mournfully gazed upon his severed wings. He had reasoned that without them, it would be easier to assume the human role, and it had most certainly helped, but that was before they began to speak to him.

With a trembling hand, the fallen angel gently stroked the downy soft surface of the wings and a faint smell of decay wafted up from them. He knew that it was impossible for the appendages to actually communicate with him, and defined the oddity as fallout from his attempt at being human. He had seen talk shows about situations just like this. The experts would say that he was delusional. Alastor smiled. To be human and insane; he had achieved far more success than he ever imagined.

"Put us on," the wings whispered seductively. *"Shed the grotesque shell that adorns you and wear us again."*

Alastor began to close the wrappings.

"What are you doing?" they asked, panic in their sound.

"I have done as you asked," he responded to his psychosis, continuing to place the sheets of plastic over the severed limbs of flight. "I can do no more than that."

"Please," the wings begged as he began to close the box.

His body wracked with guilt, Alastor ignored the plaintive cries. "I'm sorry," he managed.

The angel secured the box and stepped quickly back, listening for the sounds of protest that did not come. *Perhaps they are honoring their bargain after all.* He turned from the table, longing for the comfort of his chair, the television, and a large slice of pie. He smiled. *It's odd how much better things always are with pie.*

The laughter seemed to come from all around him.

Alastor whirled, startled by the harshness of the sound. His eyes immediately went to the box, but something told him that the sound did not come from there. Had his psychosis manifested in another way, or was he no longer alone? The angel's mind raced as he scanned the cluttered basement area before him.

A figure clad in crimson armor emerged from behind the curtain of coats hanging on pipes that ran across the cellar ceiling. Alastor gasped. The way the figure moved—stealthy and silent, almost as if he were watching something created by the madness of his own mind. Was it possible? Had his troubled thoughts created this specter in red? Something else to torment him?

But then it spoke, pointing a gauntlet-covered hand. "You try to hide, covering your pretty angel stink with the smell of man." The crimson figure shook its helmeted head, an odd clicking sound escaping from beneath the face mask. "You don't do the magick, and you cut away your wings," the man said, making a hacking gesture with one of his armored hands.

"The Powers . . . ," Alastor croaked, forcing the words from his corpulent mouth. "You serve the Powers."

He knew the answer, even before the figure clad in armor the color of blood nodded. He knew, for senses long atrophied had kicked in, the scent of Heaven's most aggressive host filling his nostrils with its fetid aroma of bloodshed.

"And you've come for me?"

Again the creature nodded.

Alastor studied the agent of the Powers, a part of him marveling at the beauty of the fearsome suit of metal that adorned his foe. The armor had been forged by Heaven's hands, of that there was no doubt. The faint light thrown by the cellar's single bulb played lovingly off the intricate details of the metal skin; it made him remember days long past, of brethren that died beneath his sword, of his fall from grace.

Panic gripped the fallen angel. He did not want to die. From within he summoned a glimmer of strength, a spark of angelic fury untapped since he had fought beside the Son of the Morning. In his mind he saw an ax and tried to bring it into the world.

The spark of heavenly fire exploded to life in the palm of his hand—and Alastor began to scream. It had been so long that it burned him. His flesh had become as that of a human, and the fires of Heaven began to consume the delicate skin. The stench of frying meat filled the basement, and the fallen angel perversely realized that he was hungry, his swollen stomach grumbling to be fed.

He tried to concentrate on the weapon he saw in his mind's eye: a battle-ax like one he had wielded in the war. In his charred hand the flames began to take shape, and Alastor felt a wave of optimism the likes of which he had not felt since devising the plan that almost made him human. He brandished the ax, fearsome and complete, at his attacker.

The figure in red giggled; an eerie sound made all the more strange filtered through the mask that hid his face.

"You find me amusing, slave of the Powers host?" Alastor asked, attempting to block out the throbbing pain in his burned hand. "We'll see how comical I am when my ax takes your head from your shoulders."

Again the armored warrior laughed, reminding Alastor of some demented child. They continued to stare at each other across the cellar space, the fires of Heaven still burning in the fallen angel's fragile grasp. The pale, doughy skin of his arm had begun to bubble and smolder. The pain was excruciating, but it helped him to focus.

"You gave it all up for this?" the red-armored horror asked, looking around at the clutter of the basement before turning his gaze back to Alastor.

The eyes within the helmet were intense, boring into his own like daggers of ice. The servant to the Powers shook his head slowly in disgust.

This act of condescension only served to inflame Alastor's rage all the more. *How dare this lowly servant look down upon me? Does he not realize the courage and fortitude my sacrifice has required?*

From deep within, Alastor dredged up the final remnants of what remained of his long inactive angelic traits. The fallen angel bellowed his disdain and threw his massive bulk across the cellar floor, scattering his accumulated belongings in his wake. He hefted the battle-ax of fire above his head, ready to cleave his enemy in twain. The flaming ax descended, passing through the coats and sports jackets that hung from the ceiling pipes, and continuing its destructive course into a musty, cardboard box filled with pots and pans.

The fallen angel spun himself around, the burning ax handle still clutched in his blackened grasp. The flaming weapon decimated a box of letters and tax records, sending burning pieces of paper up into the air, then drifting down upon him like burning snow. But despite the savagery of his assault, the weapon had yet to find its mark.

Through the burning refuse Alastor scanned the cellar in search of his adversary, weapon ready to strike yet again. He found the armored man standing before the worktable, his scarlet glove resting atop the box that contained the precious wings.

"How much did it hurt, Alastor?" the invader asked. "How great was the pain to murder what you were?"

Alastor relived the shrieking agony as he hacked his beautiful wings from his back; how he had blacked out after cutting away the first, only to return to consciousness and do away with the other. The pain had been excruciating, and was second only to his betrayal of the Creator.

The sight of the armored creature near his wings stoked the fires of his fury to maddening heights. Barely able to contain his rage, Alastor propelled himself at the figure, a cry like that of a hungry hawk erupting from his open mouth as he moved with a speed contrary to his bulk. He lifted the flaming ax above his head, but unexpectedly the intruder surged forward to meet his attack. The warrior struck quickly, fiercely, and just as fast leaped out of the fallen angel's path.

Alastor crashed into the long, wooden worktable, practically ripping it from the granite wall. The box fell, and he watched it open, spilling its precious contents as he slowly turned to face his attacker. The armored intruder stood perfectly still, his cold, predator's gaze watching him.

A terrible numbness had begun to spread from his chest, traveling to all his extremities. Alastor gazed down at his body gone to seed with the sweet indulgences of humanity, and saw the pommel of an ornate knife sticking out from the center of his chest. His strength suddenly leaving him, he watched helplessly as the ax of fire fell from his grasp to evaporate in a flash before it could hit the floor.

"What . . . what have you done to me?"

The fearsome figure shrugged its shoulders of metal. "Pretty little symbols etched into the metal of the blade," he said, drawing the same symbols in the air with his finger. "Symbols to take away strength—to make you easier to kill."

His legs no longer capable of supporting his enormous mass, Alastor pitched forward atop his wings. The aroma of their rot choked his senses, and he was overcome with a crushing sense of loss.

"I'm so sorry," he whispered to them through the plastic cover. He felt his body being turned and gazed up into the disturbing visage that straddled him.

"How? . . ." Alastor slurred, the magicks carved upon the knife blade affecting even his ability to speak.

His attacker reached down, taking hold of the knife that protruded from the center of Alastor's body.

"How?" the attacker asked, gripping the hilt.

"How did . . . how did you find me?" Alastor gasped.

The figure standing over him again began to laugh, that horrible sound of a demented child. "Find you?" it repeated, exerting pressure on the blade, cutting down through the flesh and bone of the fallen angel's chest. He completed his jagged incision, then extracted the blade and replaced it somewhere beneath the layers of his armor. "We did not need to find you," the Powers' servant said as it dug the fingers of both hands into the wound. "We knew where you were all along."

Alastor closed his eyes to his inevitable fate, focusing all his attention on the rapid-fire beating of his heart. It reminded him of the sound of flight, of his beautiful wings as they beat against the air.

And then what Alastor had sacrificed so much to keep was stolen away as the visage of death clad in scarlet tore his still-beating heart from his chest.

chapter one

"Can I take your order, sir?" asked the cute girl with the blond ponytail and a smile wide enough to split her face in two.

Aaron Corbet shook himself from his reverie and tried to focus on the menu board behind her. "Uh, yeah, thanks," he said, attempting to generate interest in yet another fast-food order. His eyes were strained from hours of driving, and the writing on the menu blurred as he tried to read it. "Give me a Whopper-with-cheese value meal, and four large fries to go."

Aaron hoped the four orders of fries would be enough to satisfy Camael's strange new craving for the greasy fast food. Just a few days ago the angel had given him a song and dance about how creatures of Heaven didn't need to eat—but that had been before he sampled some of the golden fried potatoes. *Angels addicted to French fries,* Aaron thought with a wry shake of his head. *Who'da thunk it?*

But then again, who could have predicted this crazy turn his life had taken? he thought as he waited for his order to be filled. The angel Camael had become his companion and mentor since Aaron's realization that he was born a Nephilim. He remembered how insane it had all sounded at first—the hybrid offspring of the mating between a human woman and an angelic being. Aaron thought he was losing his mind. And then people he cared about started dying, and he realized there was much more at stake than just his sanity.

Aaron turned away from the counter and looked out over the dining room. He noticed a couple with a little boy who appeared to be no more than four years old. The child was playing with a blue plastic top that he must have gotten as a prize with his kid's meal. Aaron immediately thought of Stevie, his foster brother, and a weighty feeling of unease washed over him. He recalled the last time he had seen his little brother. The seven-year-old autistic child was being dragged from their home in the clutches of an angel—a soldier in the service of a murderous host of angels called the Powers. The Powers wanted Aaron dead, for he was not just a Nephilim, he was also supposed to be the chosen one spoken of in an angelic prophecy written over a millennium ago, promising redemption to the fallen angels.

At first it had been an awful lot to swallow, but lately Aaron had begrudgingly come to accept the bizarre twists and turns that life seemed to have in store for him. Camael said that it was all part of his destiny, which had been predetermined long before he was born.

The child had managed to make the top spin and, much to his parents' amusement, clapped his hands together as the plastic toy careened about the table top.

The prophecy predicted that someone very much like Aaron would be responsible for bringing forgiveness to the angels hiding on Earth since the Great War in Heaven, that he would be the one to reunite the fallen with God. It's a big job for an eighteen-year old foster kid from Lynn, Massachusetts, but who was he to argue with destiny?

The spinning top flew from the table and the little boy began to scream in panic. Again Aaron was bombarded with painful memories of the recent past, of his foster brother's cries as he was stolen away. "I think I'll keep him," the Powers leader, Verchiel, had said as he handled the little boy like some kind of house pet. Aaron's blood seethed with the memory. Perhaps he *was* some kind of savior, but there was nothing he wanted more than to find his brother. Everything else would have to wait until Stevie was safe again.

The child continued to wail while his panicked parents scrambled to find the lost toy. On hands and knees the boy's father retrieved the top from beneath a nearby table and brought the child's sadness to an abrupt end by returning the toy to him. Though his face was still streaked with tears, the boy was smiling broadly now. *If only my task could be as simple,* Aaron thought wearily.

"Do you want ketchup?" he heard someone say close by, as he turned his thoughts to how much farther he'd be able to drive tonight. He was tired, and for a brief moment he considered teaching Camael how to drive, but that thought was stricken from his mind by the image of the heavenly warrior in the midst of a minor traffic altercation, cutting another driver in two with a flaming sword.

Aaron felt a hand upon his shoulder and spun around to see the girl with the ponytail and the incredibly wide smile holding out his bags of food. "Ketchup?" she asked again.

"Were you talking to me?" he asked, embarrassed, as he took the bags. "I'm sorry, I'm just a bit dazed from driving all day and . . ."

He froze. His foster mom would have described the strange feeling as somebody walking over his grave, whatever the hell that meant. He never did understand the strange superstitions she often shared, but for some reason, the imagery of that one always stuck with him. Aaron missed his foster parents, who had been mercilessly slain by Verchiel, and it made his desire to find his brother all the more urgent. He turned away from the counter to see a man hurriedly going out a back door, two others in pursuit.

The angelic nature that had been a part of him since his eighteenth birthday screamed to be noticed, and senses far beyond the human norm kicked into action. There was a trace of something in the air that marked the men's passing as they left the store. It was an aroma that Aaron could discern even over the prominent smells of hot vegetable oil and frying meat. The air was tainted with the rich smell of spice—and of blood.

With a polite thank-you he took his food and left the store, quickly heading to the metallic blue Toyota Corolla parked at the back of the lot. He could see the eager face of his dog in the back window. Gabriel began to bark happily as he reached the car, not so much that his master had returned, but that he had returned with food.

"What took so long?" the dog asked as Aaron placed the bags on the driver's seat. *"I didn't think you were ever coming out."*

Being able to understand and speak any form of language, including the vocalizations of animals, was yet another strange manifestation of Aaron's angelic talents, and one that was both a blessing and a curse when it came to his canine friend.

"I'm starved, Aaron," the dog said eagerly, hoping that there would be something in one of

the bags to satisfy what seemed to be a Labrador retriever's insatiable urge to eat.

Gabriel also loved to talk, and after Aaron had used his unique abilities to save the dog after a car accident, the Lab had suddenly become much smarter, making him quite the dynamic personality. Aaron loved the dog more than just about anything else, but there were days that he wished Gabriel was *only* a dog.

"I'd really like to eat," he said from the backseat, licking his chops.

"Not now, Gabe," Aaron responded, directing his attention to the large man sitting with his eyes closed in the passenger seat. "I have to speak with Camael." The angel ignored him, but that didn't stop Aaron from talking. "Inside the restaurant," he said. "I think three angels just went out the back door and . . ."

Camael slowly turned his head and opened his steely blue eyes. "Two of them are of the Powers; the other, a fallen angel"—he tilted back his head of silvery white hair and sniffed, the mustache of his goatee twitching—"of the host Cherubim, I believe. I was aware of their presence when we pulled into the lot."

"And you didn't think it was important to say anything?" Aaron asked, annoyed. "This could be the break we've been waiting for. They might know where Stevie is."

The angel stared at him without emotion, the plight of Aaron's little brother obviously the furthest thing from his mind. With Camael, it was all about fulfilling the prophecy—that and finding a mysterious haven for fallen angels called Aerie.

"We have to go after them," Aaron said forcefully. "This is the first contact we've had with anything remotely angelic since we left Maine."

Gabriel stuck his head between the front seats. *"Then we really should eat first. Right, Camael?"* he asked, eyeing the bags resting on the seat. *"Can't go after angels on an empty stomach, that's what I always say."* The dog had begun to drool, spattering the emergency break.

Camael moved his arm so as not to be splashed and glared at the animal. "I do not need to eat," he snarled, apparently very sensitive to the recent craving he had developed for French fries.

Aaron opened the back door of the car and motioned for Gabriel to get out. "C'mon," he said to them both. "We have to hurry or we'll lose them."

"May I have a few fries before we go?" the dog asked as he leaped from the car to the parking lot. *"Just to hold me over until we get back."*

Aaron ignored his dog and slammed the door closed, anxious to be on his way.

"Do you think this wise?" Camael asked as he removed himself from the front seat of the car. "To draw attention to ourselves in such a way?"

Aaron knew there was a risk in confronting the angels, but if they were ever going to find his brother they had to take the chance. "The Powers answer to Verchiel, and he's the one who took Stevie," Aaron said, hoping that the angel would understand. "I don't think I could live with myself if I didn't at least try to find out what they know."

Camael moved around the car casually buttoning his dark suit jacket, impeccable as always. "You do realize that this will likely end in death."

"Tell me something I don't know," Aaron said as he turned away from his companions and followed the dwindling trail of angel scents into the dense woods behind the fast-food restaurant.

No matter how he tried to distract himself, Verchiel found himself drawn to the classroom within the St. Athanasius Orphanage where the prisoner was held.

Standing in the shadows of the room, the angel stared at the huddled figure feigning sleep within his prison, and marveled at how a mere cage of iron could contain an evil so vast. Verchiel would destroy the prisoner if he could, but even he was loath to admit that he did not have the power to accomplish such a task. He would have to take a level of satisfaction from the evil one's containment, at least for now. When matters with the Nephilim and the accursed prophecy were properly settled, then he could concentrate on an appropriate punishment for the captive.

"Am I that fascinating a specimen?" the prisoner asked from his cage. He slowly brought himself to a sitting position, his back against the bars. In his hand he held a gray furred mouse and gently stroked its tiny skull with an index finger. "I don't believe we saw this much of each other when we still lived in Heaven."

Verchiel bristled at the mention of his former home; it had been too long since last he looked upon its glorious spires and the memory of its beauty was almost too painful to bear. "Those were different times," he said coldly. "And we . . . different beings." The leader of the Powers suddenly wanted to leave the room, to be away from the criminal responsible for so much misery, but he stayed, both revolted and mesmerized by the fallen angel and all he had come to embody.

"Call me crazy," the prisoner said conversationally as he gestured with his chin beyond the confines of his prison, "but even locked away in here I can feel that something is happening."

Verchiel found himself drawn toward the cage. "Go on."

"You know how it feels before a summer storm?" the prisoner asked. "How the air is charged with an energy that tells you something big is on the way? That's how it feels to me. That something really big is coming." The prisoner continued to pet the vermin's head, waiting for some kind of confirmation. "Well, what do you think, Verchiel?" he asked. "Is there a storm on the way?"

The angel could not help but boast. His plans were reaching fruition and he felt confident. "More deluge than storm," Verchiel responded as he turned his back upon the captive. "When the Nephilim—this Aaron Corbet—is finally put down, a time of change will be upon us." He strode to a haphazardly boarded window and peered through the cracks at the New England summer night with eyes that saw through darkness as if it were day.

"With the savior of their blasphemous prophecy dead, all of the unpunished criminals of the Great War, driven to despair by the realization that their Lord of Lords will *not* forgive them, will at last be hunted down and executed." Verchiel turned from the window to gaze at his prize. "That is what you are feeling in the air, Son of the Morning. The victory of the Powers—my victory."

The prisoner brought the mouse up to his mouth and gently laid a kiss upon its tiny pointed head. "If you say so, but it doesn't feel like that to me. Feels more special than that," he said. The mouse nuzzled his chin and the prisoner chuckled, amused by the tiny creature's show of affection.

Verchiel glided toward the cage, a cold smile forming on his colorless lips. "And what could be more special than the Nephilim dying at the hands of his sibling?" he asked the prisoner cruelly. "We have spared nothing in our pursuit to destroy him."

The prisoner shook his head disapprovingly. "You're going to use this kid's brother to kill him? That's cold, Verchiel—even for someone with my reputation."

The angel smiled, pleased by the twisted compliment. "The child was a defective, a burden to the world in which he was born—that is, until I transformed him, forged him into a weapon with only one purpose: to kill the Nephilim and every tainted ideal that he represents." He paused for dramatic effect, studying the expression of unease upon the captive's gaunt face. "Cold?" Verchiel asked. "Most assuredly, for to bring about the end of this conflict I must be the coldest one there is."

The mouse had defecated in the prisoner's hand and he casually wiped it upon his robe of heavy brown cloth. "What makes this Nephilim—this Aaron Corbet—any different from the thousands of others you've killed over the millennia?"

Verchiel recalled his battle with this supposed savior, the ancient angelic sigils that covered his flesh, his ebony wings, the savagery of his combat skills. "There is nothing special about this one," he sneered. "And those of the fallen who cling to the belief that he is the savior of prophecy must be shown this."

He remembered how they battled within the storm he himself had conjured, weapons of heavenly fire searing the very air. It was to be a killing blow; his sword of fire poised to sever the blasphemer's head from his body. And then, inexplicably, lightning struck at Verchiel, and he fell from the sky in flames. The burns on his body had yet to heal, the pain a constant reminder of the Nephilim, and how much was at stake. "With his death," Verchiel continued, "they will be shown that the prophecy is a lie, that there will be no forgiveness from the Creator."

The prisoner leaned his head of shaggy black hair against the iron bars of his prison as the mouse crawled freely in his lap. "Why does the idea of the prophecy threaten you so?" he asked. "After all this time, is absolution such a terrible thing?"

Verchiel felt his anger blaze. His mighty wings unfurled from his back, stirring the dust and stagnant air of the room. "It is an affront to God! Those who fought against the Lord of Lords should be punished for their crimes, not forgiven."

The prisoner closed his eyes. "But think of it, Verchiel: to have the past cleared away. Personally I think it would be pretty sweet." He opened his eyes and smiled a beatific smile that again reminded Verchiel of how it had been in Heaven—and how much had been lost to them all. "Who knows," the prisoner added, "it might even clear up that complexion of yours."

It was a notion that had crossed Verchiel's mind as well—that his lack of healing was a sign that the Creator was not pleased with his actions—but to have it suggested by one so vilified, so foul, was enough to test his sanity. The leader of the Powers surged toward the cage, grabbing the bars of iron.

"If I have incurred the wrath of my heavenly sire, it is for what I failed to do, rather than what I have done." Verchiel felt the power of his angelic glory course through his body, down his arms, and into his hands. "I did not succeed in killing the Nephilim, but I have every intention of correcting that oversight."

The metal of the cage began to glow a fiery orange with the heat of heavenly fire, and the prisoner moved to its center. His robes and the soles of his sandals began to smolder. "I deserve this," he said, a steely resolve in his dark eyes. "But *he* doesn't." He held the mouse out toward Verchiel and moved to the bars that now glowed a yellowish white. He thrust his arm between the barriers, his sleeve immediately bursting into flame, and let the mouse fall to the floor where it scurried off to hide among the shadows.

"How touching," Verchiel said, continuing to feed his unearthly energies into the metal bars of the prison. "It fills me with hope to see one as wicked as you showing such concern for one of the Father's lowliest creatures."

"It's called compassion, Verchiel," the prisoner said though gritted teeth, his simple clothing ablaze. "A divine trait, and one that you are severely lacking."

"How dare you," Verchiel growled, shaking the bars of the cage that now burned with a white-hot radiance. "I am, if nothing else, a spark of all that is the Creator; an extension of His divinity upon the world."

The prisoner fell, his body burning, his blackening skin sending wisps of oily smoke into the air as he writhed upon the blistering hot floor of the cage. "But what if it's true, Verchiel?" he asked in an impossibly calm voice. "What if . . . it's all part of His plan?"

"Blasphemy!" the angel bellowed, his anger making the bars burn all the brighter—all the hotter. "Do you seriously think that the Creator can forgive those who tried to usurp His reign?"

"I've heard tell," the prisoner whispered through lips blistered and oozing, "that He does work in mysterious ways."

Verchiel was enjoying his captive's suffering. "And what if it *is* true, Morningstar? What if the prophecy is some grand scheme of amnesty composed by God? Do you actually believe that *you* would be forgiven?"

The prisoner had curled into a tight ball, the flesh of his body aflame, but still he answered. "If I were to believe in the prophecy . . . then it would be up to the Nephilim . . . wouldn't it?"

"Yes," Verchiel answered. "Yes, it would. And it will never be allowed to happen."

The prisoner lifted his head, any semblance of discernable features burned away. "Is that why I'm here?" he croaked in a dry whisper. "Is that why you've captured me . . . locked me away . . . so that I will never be given that chance?"

Verchiel sent a final burst of energy through the metal of the cage. The prisoner thrashed like a fish pulled from a stream and tossed cruelly upon the land. Then he grew very still, the intensity of his injuries sending him into the embrace of unconsciousness.

The Powers' leader released the bars and stepped back. He knew that his captive would live, it would take far more than he could conjure to destroy something so powerful, but the injuries would cause him to suffer, and that was acceptable for now.

Verchiel turned from the cage and walked toward the door. There was still much to be done; he had no more time to concern himself with prisoners of war.

"As does the Lord," he said to himself, "I too work in mysterious ways."

The power of Heaven, tainted by the poison of arrogance and insanity, flowed through his injured body, bringing with it the most debilitating pain—but also sweet oblivion.

The prisoner drifted in a cold sea of darkness and dreamed.

In his dreams he saw a boy, and somehow he knew that this was the Nephilim of prophecy. There was nothing special about the way he looked, or the way he carried himself, but the Powers captive knew that this was the One—this was Aaron Corbet. The boy was moving purposefully through a thicket of woods; and he wasn't alone. Deep within the womb of unconsciousness the prisoner smiled as he saw an angel walking at the boy's side.

Camael, he thought, remembering how he had long ago called the warrior "friend." But that was before the jealousy, before the war, before the fall.

And then he saw the dog; it had gone ahead into the woods, but now returned to tell its master what it had found. It was a beautiful animal, its fur the color of the purest sunshine. It loved its master, he could tell by the way it moved around the boy, the way it cocked its head as it communicated, the way its tail wagged.

It would be easy to like this boy, the prisoner guessed as the sharp pain of his injuries began to intrude upon his insensate state. He pulled himself deeper into the healing embrace of the void. *How could I not like someone who has caused Verchiel such distress?* the prisoner wondered. And besides, Aaron Corbet had a dog.

I've always been a sucker for dogs.

chapter two

Johiel was annoyed with Earth the moment he arrived over a millenium ago, but as the toe of his sneaker caught beneath an unearthed root, and he fell sprawling, face first to the forest floor, the fallen angel felt his simple antipathy ripen to bitter hatred. He hit the ground hard, the air punched from his lungs in a wheezing grunt, and slid halfway down a small embankment before regaining enough of his composure to struggle to his feet. Yes, Johiel hated living upon the Earth. However, the alternative—far more permanent—was even less appealing.

He chanced a look behind him to see if they were still following. What a foolish thought. *They are soldiers of the Powers; of course they're still following.* The ground beneath his feet started to level off and in the distance he could hear the sounds of cars and trucks as they traveled along the highway. *I can make it to the road*, he thought, his mind abuzz. *Perhaps I can hitch a ride and escape*.

Stumbling through the darkness of the woods, Johiel chastised himself for his rabid stupidity. If he hadn't tried to make contact with the Powers, he would not be in this predicament. How could he have been so foolish as to think that they could be convinced to show even the slightest leniency toward their enemies, no matter what was offered? But he had grown so tired of living in fear; a constant cloud of oppression hanging over his head, never knowing which moment would be his last.

The sounds of the road were closer now and he began to think that they had grown tired of the pursuit. Perhaps they decided he just wasn't worth the effort, he thought, both relieved and a little insulted that the Powers wouldn't even attempt to learn the information he wanted to trade for his life. Johiel was certain that his knowledge would prove valuable to their leader, and he would have given it freely for a chance to live without fear.

The ground before him suddenly exploded in a roiling ball of fire, and Johiel was thrown backward to the cool, moist forest floor.

"Is it something we said, little fallen brother?" said a cold, cruel voice behind him.

"Or something we didn't say, perhaps?" asked another, equally malevolent.

Johiel scrambled to his feet and turned to see two immaculately dressed and smiling angels strolling through the woods toward him. He knew he had three choices, two of which would likely end in his own excruciating demise: He could run and be cut down like a lowly animal; he could fight and perish just the same; or he could carry through with his original plan. The notion of engaging the two Powers in conversation was terrifying, but he held his ground and summoned a sword of fire to defend himself if it proved necessary.

The warriors stopped in unison, the sparking flame of Johiel's weapon reflecting off the inky blackness of their eyes.

"I do not understand, Bethmael," said one to the other. "The criminal put word out that he wished to speak with us, yet flees when we approach. And now he brandishes a weapon?"

Bethmael sneered. "It is the world, brother Kyriel," he said, continuing to stare at the fallen angel. "They know they do not belong here, and the knowledge drives them mad."

Their wings gracefully expanded from their backs, reminding Johiel of king cobras unfurling their hoods before they strike.

"I wanted to speak with a representative of the Powers," he built up the courage to say. "Someone who has Lord Verchiel's ear. But instead I am attacked and forced to flee for my life."

Kyriel's wings languidly flapped and a sword sprang to life in his hand, lighting the darkened wood like dawn. "And what could a criminal possibly have to say that might interest Lord Verchiel?"

"I have information," Johiel began, suddenly unsure. The idea of betraying those who had once welcomed him into their fold filled him with trepidation, but not enough to hold his tongue. "The location of the place that you have desperately sought, but still cannot find."

"You wish an exchange of some kind?" Bethmael asked.

His large hands remained free of weapons and Johiel watched him with cautious eyes. He did not trust the Powers, but this was his last chance to be free of the fear that had plagued him since the war. He would either be free, or he would be dead.

"An exchange for my life," he explained. "I will give you the location of the secret haven, and you will grant me freedom."

"You're asking for immunity from our righteous wrath?" Kyriel asked, lowering his own mighty sword of fire.

"For what I give you, the life of one fallen angel is a bargain," Johiel answered.

The two Powers looked at each other, a communication passing between their gazes. Kyriel again raised his weapon. "Our fallen brother attempts to barter for his life," he said to

Bethmael, bemused. Bethmael nodded, a humorless smile appearing on his beatific features. "Protection in exchange for information."

They were both smiling now, and Johiel began to believe that his gambit had actually paid off. He wished his weapon away as a sign of good faith, but he could not help thinking again of those who would die so that he could live. *I'll learn to live with that,* he thought. "Your word is your bond," he said aloud to Bethmael and Kyriel. "Do we have a deal?"

They laughed, a shrill, high-pitched sound that conjured images of a bird of prey as it dropped from the sky upon its kill. Johiel should have seen this for the warning that it was.

"The Powers do not bargain with criminals," Bethmael said as a weapon—a longbow—formed in his grasp, and in a matter of seconds he let fly a shaft of fire. It hissed as it cut through the air, as if warning its target of the excruciating pain of its bite.

The arrow of fire plunged deep into the flesh of Johiel's shoulder, the momentum carrying him backward, pinning him to the body of an ancient oak. Frantically Johiel tried to free himself. He gripped the shaft and the night air was suddenly filled with the sickly sweet fragrance of burning flesh. He screamed pathetically as he pulled his blistered hand away. Through eyes tearing with pain, he watched the two angels stalk closer.

"It is our turn to make a bargain with you, fallen one," Bethmael said. His bow had already been replaced with a dagger of fire that he held menacingly before Johiel. "You will tell us your secrets, and then you will be killed mercifully."

Johiel struggled to pull his shoulder from the tree, but the pain was too great. "I . . . I'll tell you nothing," he said, voice trembling with fear and agony. The fire of the arrow was beginning to eat at the flesh of his shoulder, beginning to spread voraciously down his arm.

"I was so hoping you would say that," Kyriel said, a knife coming to life in his grasp as well.

Johiel didn't want to die—especially not painfully. Perhaps a taste of his secret knowledge would grant him a small respite. "I know where the fallen hide," he proclaimed as the burning blades moved toward his flesh.

Bethmael stopped and motioned for Kyriel to halt as well. "Go on," the angel urged. "Unburden yourself."

"I . . . I can take you there . . . right to their doorstep," he stammered.

"He's bluffing," Kyriel snapped, and again started forward with knife in hand.

"I could tell you where, . . . but you won't find it without my help," Johiel whined, writhing in pain as the heavenly fire of the arrow in his shoulder continued to feed upon his flesh. "It's hidden with magick, . . . but I can show you where it is."

"I grow tired of his games, brother," Kyriel said, eager to inflict more pain. "We'll cut the flesh from his traitorous bones and—"

"Silence, Kyriel," Bethmael ordered, a look forming in his black gaze that told Johiel the Powers' soldier had begun to understand the importance of what he knew. "What is this place of which you speak?" Bethmael asked with intense curiosity.

Johiel looked to the arrow protruding from his shoulder, and then back to Bethmael. "Remove the arrow, and I'll share all that I know," he said, sensing that he was suddenly worth more to them alive than dead.

"What is the name of the place of which you speak?" Bethmael asked again.

Johiel was about to tell him when a rustle of brush and the snapping of twigs distracted them all from the business at hand.

The yellow-furred dog was the first to come upon them. It stopped, cocked its head to one side, and stared with deep brown eyes showing far more intelligence than expected from the average canine. A boy was next, followed by a familiar angel. Johiel believed his name to be Camael, a great angel warrior and traitor to the Powers host.

"Told you I could find them first," the yellow dog said to the boy.

"And now that we have?" the angel warrior inquired.

The boy's appearance began to change, and Johiel thought he heard the Powers gasp. Sigils, angelic sigils appeared upon the boy's flesh. It was then that Johiel realized this was much more than a mere boy.

"And now that we've found them," the boy repeated, his voice dropping to a rumbling growl, "we kick their asses until they tell us what we want to know."

"I urge caution," Camael said quietly, placing his hand on Aaron's shoulder. "Enter into battle without prudence, and have no one but yourself to blame for an untimely death."

Camael eyed the scene before him. It was typical: two agents of the Powers preparing to dispatch yet another fallen angel for crimes against Heaven. How many had died by his own hands in service to the Powers and their sacred mission, before he realized that the dispensing of death was not the answer.

"All right," Aaron said, impatience in his tone. "I'm being cautious. I haven't attacked yet—but how long should I be cautious before I get to kick butt?"

The two Powers stepped away from their prey, spreading their wings and puffing out their broad warriors' chests. The knives they each held changed, growing in size to something more formidable, something far more deadly.

"Do my eyes deceive me, brother Kyriel?" asked one soldier to the other. "Or is that former commander Camael I see before me?"

Camael was familiar with both Kyriel and Bethmael. They had served him well in his time as leader of the Powers host. It saddened him now to see the glint of madness in their eyes.

"But how can that be, Bethmael?" Kyriel asked mockingly. "The great Camael left the ways of violence to ascend to a higher level of being. I hear tell that he has taken up sides with a savior of sorts, a divine creature with the ability to bend the ear of God."

"Do tell," said Bethmael in response. "Then I am sorely mistaken, for those who stand before us now are neither higher beings nor saviors of any kind."

Camael would have welcomed a chance to explain his change of heart, his altered philosophy clarified by the reading of an ancient prophecy that foretold the coming of a Nephilim. This spawn of angel and mortal woman would bring absolution to those that had fled Heaven after the war. But he knew, in the core of his being, that the soldiers of the Powers would not listen. They had been changed over the millennia, poisoned by their mission of murder under the leadership of Verchiel.

"So you know these two, huh?" Aaron asked, still obliging Camael's warning of caution.

"They once served beneath me," he answered, his gaze never leaving the angelic soldiers. He recalled that the two had been ferocious warriors, their dedication to the cause unwavering. They would be formidable opponents indeed.

Bethmael pointed his awesome sword of flame at them. "Let us show you how we deal with traitors and mongrels," he said, a goading smile on his aquiline features.

"Have you heard enough of their crap yet?" Aaron asked.

Camael brought forth a blade of his own and readied himself for battle. "I believe I have."

Aaron suddenly turned to face him, placing a sigil-covered hand upon his chest. "Let me do this," he said forcefully. The young man's eyes glinted wetly, like two black pearls in a sea of unbridled emotion. "I have to learn to control it, you've said so yourself."

He could not argue with the boy, for it was what he had been attempting to teach Aaron all along. The angelic nature of the Nephilim was often a dangerous and tempestuous force. The human animal was not meant to wield such power, and it often drove them insane. Camael tried to recall the number of Nephilim driven mad by the power of their own angelic nature that he had been forced to put down. There were far more than he cared to remember.

"Don't worry," Aaron said confidently. "I'll give a yell if I need a hand."

The boy turned away and flexed his shoulders. Powerful wings of shiny black feathers sprouted from his back, tearing through his

T-shirt. In his hand a sword of orange flame appeared and he hurled himself at the angelic opponents with a cry of abandon.

The power that resided within this boy was different than any other Camael had borne witness to; there was an intensity to it, something that hinted at the potential for greatness—or something devastatingly destructive. It was this that set him apart from the others, that made Camael believe that Aaron Corbet was indeed the one foretold of in prophecy, the one who could unite all of the fallen angels with Heaven. *Perhaps even . . .* He cut that thought off before it could go any further.

Camael watched with a cautious eye as the Nephilim touched down before the Powers warriors. "Let me show you how I deal with a coupla assholes," he heard the boy say, goading the angels to attack.

At first the teenager had been afraid of his talents, but now Aaron was using his new abilities more and more frequently. Camael hoped that he would soon see the unification of human and angelic in the boy—and not a gradual descent into madness. He wished this not only for the sake of the boy, but for all fallen angels hiding on Earth, hungry for reunification with God and the kingdom of Heaven.

Bethmael was first to attack, bringing his blade down in a blazing arc, crackling and sparking as it cut through the air. Aaron spread wide his ebony wings and pushed off from the ground, evading the weapon as it bit into the underbrush and set it aflame.

"Fast, but not fast enough," the Nephilim said, lashing out with his own sword of fire. The blade cut a burning gash across Bethmael's chest and the angel cried out in shock and dismay.

Eyes riveted to the scene unfolding before him, Camael suddenly felt Gabriel's presence by his side.

"I'm afraid," the dog said.

"Not to worry," Camael replied reassuringly. "Aaron will be fine."

There was silence for a moment, but then the animal spoke again.

"Right now I'm not afraid for him, Camael," the dog said with a slight tremble to his usually guttural voice. "I'm afraid of him."

As he struck at his enemies and watched the surprise and fear spread across their faces, Aaron wondered again why he had ever been so afraid.

Bethmael and Kyriel stepped away from him, cautious now that he had drawn first blood. He could still hear Bethmael's blood sizzling on the blade of his weapon. It was a wonderful sound that made the power within him yowl with delight.

This angelic essence was indeed a thing to be feared, but it was part of him now, and there was nothing he could do to change that. At first he had believed that the best way to deal with it was to suppress it, to keep the alien nature that had been awakened on his eighteenth birthday locked up inside, but that proved to be nearly impossible. The power wanted to be free to fulfill its purpose, and to be perfectly honest, Aaron knew he really wasn't strong enough to deny it. Self-control had been something he'd fought to learn for years in foster care. But his first confrontation with Verchiel over the burning remains of the only people who had ever treated him like family quickly taught him that he would have to occasionally free these newfound powers to stay alive.

"What's the matter? Scared?" Aaron asked the angels, a nasty grin spreading across his face. He imagined how he must look to them, and a chill of excitement ran up and down his spine. He *wanted* them to be afraid—he *wanted* them to fear him. They were agents of Verchiel, and that was all he needed to know. They didn't seek unification and peace. Only the merciless slaughter of those they considered "beneath" themselves.

That was it. They came at him with cries that reminded him of a bird's wail: an eagle, or a hawk perhaps. Bethmael's fiery blade passed dangerously close.

"Verchiel shall have your head," he heard the angel hiss. He felt the heat of heavenly flame streak by his face as he bent himself backward to avoid its destructive touch. Then he drove his foot into the angel's stomach, kicking him away.

Kyriel, working in unison with his brother, thrust his blade of fire toward Aaron's midsection. Aaron brought his own weapon down, swatting Kyriel's lunge aside, and carried through slashing his sword across the warrior's face. The angel stumbled back with a cry of surprise, a hand clutched to his now smoldering features.

"Bet that's gonna scar," Aaron taunted, feeling the ancient energy that he'd fought so hard to squelch course through his body. At that moment he felt as though there was nothing he couldn't do.

"He . . . he cut me," Kyriel said, gazing at the blood that covered his hand.

There wasn't much of it, the flames of the heavenly blades cauterizing the wounds, but Aaron wondered how long it had been since the angel had last seen even a little of his own blood. The Powers' soldier looked to his brother for support, though he too had been stung by Aaron's blade.

"Then we shall cut him back," Bethmael growled, spreading his wings of golden brown and springing from the ground, sword of fire ready for a taste of Nephilim blood.

Rallied by his brother, Kyriel forgot his wound and dove at Aaron.

Aaron watched them descending upon him as if in slow motion, the crackling flames of their burning swords growing louder as they drew closer. He tried to move, but found he could not. The angelic essence had grown tired of this particular battle, and was ready to bring it to an end. Aaron gave in, letting the divine power wash over him like a wave.

They were almost upon him, their angel scent filling his nostrils. There was arrogance in their stench. Even though he had held his own against their master, Verchiel, they still believed themselves superior. These angels would suffer for their conceit.

Kyriel was the first to meet his fate. His wicked blade of fire fell—its purpose to cleave Aaron in two, but the Nephilim was not there to meet the weapon's bite. With surprising speed, he moved beneath the descent of Kyriel's sword and thrust his own burning blade into the soldier's ribcage, thinking to pierce the creature's black heart.

Aaron had no time to cherish the look of sheer surprise that bled across his attacker's face for he had the other to deal with now. He turned just as Bethmael slashed a painful bite from his shoulder. But he ignored the wound, following through with his own swing. His blade passed through the thick tendrils of sinew, muscle, and bone and severed Bethmael's head from his body. Aaron watched with a perverse wonder as the angel's head spun slowly in the air before falling to the ground. The body followed, the stump where its head had once been still smoldering from the cut of his weapon.

Aaron was surprised by his feelings as he gazed down at the astonished expression, frozen upon Bethmael's dead face. There was no revulsion, no surprise. It simply felt right.

He was suddenly distracted by a moan from behind and turned to see that Kyriel was still alive. The angel knelt upon the grass, clutching at his chest, a black oily smoke drifting from his wound. He was burning from within and the expression on his face was one of unbridled pain. Aaron looked upon his attacker and he felt no pity—only a cold, efficient need to see the job done.

"Aaron," he heard Camael call from close by. He ignored his mentor and prepared to finish what he had started.

"Aaron, what are you doing?" Camael cautiously questioned as the Nephilim brought his sword of fire up, and then down upon Kyriel's skull, ending his life and bringing the battle to a close.

He felt Camael's hand fall roughly upon his shoulder, spinning him around to face his mentor. There was a split second when the power inside told him to lift his blade against the angel, but he managed to suppress the urge as he slowly emerged from the red haze of combat.

Camael was looking at him, eyes wide with

dismay, although Aaron wasn't altogether sure what he had done to garner such a reaction. "What's the matter?" he asked, feeling the sigils upon his body start to fade, the wings upon his back furl beneath the flesh.

Gabriel had joined the angel and was looking up at him with an equal expression of shock. *"You killed them, Aaron,"* the dog said, disappointment in his tone.

"I did at that," Aaron replied, a smile tugging at the corners of his mouth as he remembered the remarkable feeling of letting the power inside him take control. "Bet they didn't think I'd be able to—"

"But how are they going to help us find Stevie?" Gabriel asked, and Aaron felt the world give way beneath him. He hadn't even thought of his brother during the fury of battle.

"What have I done?" he whispered, refusing to look at the accusatory gazes of his friends. Aaron focused his stare on the smoldering bodies of those he had vanquished, the horror of what he had done in the throes of battle, and what he had carelessly forgotten just then beginning to sink in.

And the power inside him rested, satisfied.

Sated for now.

The hot orange flames burned higher and fiercer as they fed upon the corpses of the Powers' soldiers. Aaron could not pull his gaze from the sight as the unnatural fire consumed them, any chance of them sharing information about Stevie's fate silenced in a moment of gratuitous violence.

"What's wrong with me, Camael?" he asked as he watched the bones of angels burn to powder. "I didn't even think of Stevie," he said sadly. "It was like he didn't even matter."

"The power that is inside you can be a selfish thing," the angel said coldly. "It cares only to satisfy its needs. It is a wild thing and must be tamed. There must be unity between the human and angelic, or there can be only chaos."

A skull popped like a gunshot as it collapsed in upon itself in an explosion of fiery embers.

"I thought that when the power awakened in me . . . and when I talked to it that . . ."

"That was only the beginning of a much longer and difficult process," Camael said as he brushed the flying ash of his brethren from the sleeve of his suit jacket. "Unification must occur or . . ."

The angel trailed off, and Aaron finally looked away from the burning remains of the creatures he had killed. "Or what?" he asked, not sure if he really wanted to know the answer.

Camael met his gaze with eyes as cold as an arctic breeze, and Aaron felt the hair at the nape of his neck stand on end. "Or it will make you insane, and I will be forced to destroy you."

Aaron found he couldn't breathe. As if he

didn't have enough to concern him; now he had to worry about losing his mind and being killed by someone he'd grown to trust. The angelic nature inside him was awake again and it cared very little for Camael's words. It wanted to be free, to confront Camael's threat, but Aaron struggled to keep it in check, defying its need for violence.

"Do you think I'm going insane?" he asked the angel.

Camael said nothing, averting his gaze to the stars. Aaron was about to press the question when Gabriel began to bark.

"What is it?" He looked down at his dog, whose hackles had risen ominously upon his neck.

"*I think we've got more trouble,*" the dog growled menacingly, padding past them in a crouch.

Aaron and Camael turned to see two figures standing before the tree where the Powers' original prey had been pinned by an arrow of fire. In the mayhem of battle, they had forgotten about the fallen angel, and now it appeared as though he had some friends after all. There was a man, dressed as though he had just walked off the set of a spaghetti western: cowboy boots and hat, black denim and a long brown duster that flowed around him in a nonexistent breeze. The woman, in denim as well, but wearing a more contemporary style of dress, stood out in the darkness, for her long, flowing hair was the color of freshly fallen snow.

"Who are . . . ?" Aaron began as the cowboy reached out and began to pull the arrow from the fallen angel's shoulder.

"Fallen," Camael announced, his nose twitching as he sniffed the air. "And the girl is Nephilim."

The angel cried out in pain as he was released, falling to his knees at the edge of the clearing.

"Looks as though they've come to rescue their friend," Aaron said, and then stopped.

The fallen angel that had removed the burning arrow from the Powers' victim had flipped back his coat, and from somewhere on his person had produced a pistol that would have been right at home in the old West, but this one seemed to be made of gold. He stepped back, aimed at the kneeling angel, and unmercifully shot him once in the forehead.

"Oh, shit," Aaron whispered, watching as the angel slumped to the ground, dead.

"I don't think they are his friends," Camael voiced, the echo of the single gunshot gradually fading.

Gabriel immediately began to bark, and the two newcomers spun to face them.

"I'd quiet that animal," said the cowboy as he turned his aim toward them. He was tall, his weathered features lined with age, long gray hair streaming out from beneath his Stetson. "Wouldn't want to make me nervous and have my gun go off accidentally," he said with a snarl.

"Who's he calling an animal?" Gabriel asked, barking and lunging forward threateningly.

"Quiet, Gabriel," Aaron said, placing the tips of his fingers reassuringly on the dog's rump.

A sword of fire ignited beside him, and he glanced over to see that Camael was preparing himself, just in case. He felt his own inner essence exert itself, and the strange markings again seared the surface of his flesh. Reluctantly he let the power come.

"We want no trouble," Camael's voice boomed. He held his sword at the ready. "Allow us to go our way, and this will be the end of it."

The two were silent. The woman casually combed the fingers of one hand through her long white hair, and Aaron realized that she probably wasn't much older than himself.

"Were they Verchiel's?" she asked, pointing to the still-smoldering remains behind them.

"Yes," Aaron answered. His wings had emerged and he slowly unfurled them, giving the potential attackers a glimpse of what would be in store for them if they started any trouble.

"Imagine that." The angel with the pistol squinted at them. "The likes of you taking down two of Verchiel's soldiers."

"I think we should bring them in," said the woman coldly.

She was a Nephilim, and Aaron felt a certain kinship with her, but he didn't care for what he was hearing. *Bring us in? Like we're criminals, or specimens, or something.*

"We're not going anywhere," Camael warned. "This can end in one of two ways—and one is not at all in your favor."

The angel with the pistol chuckled. "Not in our favor," he said. "I like that." And then he looked to the woman. "Lorelei, take 'em down."

"Right you are, Lehash," she said, and spread her arms, a strange guttural language spilling from her mouth.

Aaron heard the words and immediately knew that things were about to turn ugly. She was casting some kind of spell, calling upon the elements. He tensed, a sword suddenly in his hand.

"Camael, we have to—"

The air roared, like the largest of jungle cats, and jagged claws of lightning dropped down from the sky upon them. There was a brilliant flash, and then everything was black.

Aaron didn't even have a chance to finish his sentence.

chapter three

Malak's arrival was heralded by a tremble of the very air. It shook years of accumulated dust and dirt from the heating pipes and ducts spreading across the ceiling of the dormant boiler room in the sub-basement of the Saint Athanasius Orphanage. And then there came a tearing sound as a rip in the fabric of space appeared in the room and grew steadily larger to allow the servant of the Powers access to his place of solitude.

The fearsome figure, clad in ornate armor the color of drying blood and carrying a dripping sack, forced his body through the laceration in the flesh of reality. The armor, forged in the fires of Heaven and bestowed upon him by the chieftain of the Powers host, allowed him this fantastic mode of transportation. In an instant he could follow a scent wherever it might take him.

As his feet hit the concrete floor of his dwelling, the hovering wound behind him revealed a place of frigid, howling winds, covered with ice and snow. Gradually it healed and soon, was no more.

Malak sniffed the air, searching for signs that anyone other than he had been within his den. The scent was all his and the hunter relaxed. He placed the satchel on the floor and pulled the helmet from his head, setting it down atop a stack of magazines tied with twine. His scalp tingled as it was exposed to the air, and he raised a gloved hand to his head, running metal-encased fingers through his shaggy blond hair. *It's good to be home,* he thought, gazing about the dank, dark room. His eyes fell upon the familiar sites: the piles of wooden desks, stacks of moldering textbooks. There were rows of file cabinets, their once important information now meaningless, and an ancient boiler, squatting in the darkness, its system of pipes and ducts reaching overhead like the tentacles of some long-extinct primordial beast. This was his place, a respite where he could gather his strength and concentrate on the hunts to come.

Home . . .

Malak retrieved his bag from the floor and headed across the sub-basement. The bag was dripping and left a serpentine trail upon the stones. He passed a dust-covered globe of the world and cheerfully gave it a spin.

Bolted to the wall at the back of the boiler room were rows of shelves that had once held supplies for the upkeep of the church buildings, but now held items of a decidedly different nature. Malak struck a match from a box and lit the candles placed about the shelves. The hunter's smile broadened as the flickering light illuminated his treasures, prizes from his hunts. He admired the leathery ears he had cut from the heads of a tribe of fallen hiding in the jungles of South America, and the glass jars with the eyes of those who did not recognize the heavenly authority of the Powers on Earth. The tongues he had pulled from the mouths of those fallen that had spoken ill of his lord and master, and the countless, bloodstained feathers he had plucked from the wings of those cast out of Heaven—all of this filled him with a burgeoning pride. *So many hunts*, he mused, recalling the death strikes to each and every one of his hapless prey.

Malak stepped closer to the shelves and pushed aside the blackened skull of a fallen angel who foolishly believed that God was by his side as he fought. He then reached into his dripping sack and removed a pair of severed hands, placing them in the space he had just cleared. In his mind he heard the screams of the angel as the appendages were taken from him only a short time ago, and he smiled, the pitiful cries of torment sweet music to his ears. He stepped back and again admired his growing collection. *Feet*, he suddenly thought. *My collection could use a pair of feet.*

Another stronger scent wafted up from the saturated bag in his hand and Malak pulled it open to peer inside. He licked his lips, feeling his stomach churn and gurgle with hunger as he gazed upon the most delectable prize still within. Carefully he withdrew the last item from the sack, the source of the soaking fluids staining its bottom—a dripping angel's heart.

"I trust your latest undertaking was a success?" said a voice from behind him, and the hunter turned quickly to gaze lovingly upon his master.

Verchiel casually strolled toward him, hands clasped behind his back, and Malak dropped to his knees, bowing his head in reverence.

"I hope I have made you proud," the hunter said.

"I am certain you did," the angel said as he walked past his kneeling servant to approach the trophy shelf.

"I see that there are many more . . . items since last I checked," Verchiel said, his eyes studying the hunter's display.

"Every day I hunt," Malak replied. "Sometimes two or three of the criminals die at my hand. I like the trophies to remind me of the glory of the moment."

"You most certainly do," Verchiel clucked,

turning away from the shelves to look upon him. "And the scent of the Nephilim? Have you found it again?"

Malak bowed his head again, not wanting to endure the look of disappointment in his master's eyes. Two weeks ago he had found the scent of the half-breed in the lair of the sea beast. There had been a great battle there, and the Nephilim had stained the rocks with his blood. But Malak soon lost the trail. The Nephilim and his companion were taking no chances, masking their travels with powerful magicks.

"I have not," Malak said sadly. "But it is only a matter of time before I pick up the trail again and track him down—to the ends of the world if necessary."

Verchiel chuckled. "I'm sure you will, faithful Malak, but do not fret." The angel smiled down on him and the hunter was bathed in its radiance. "Losing the scent of our enemy has provided you with an opportunity to hone your special skills." He gestured toward the shelves filled with Malak's trophies. "Think of these as steps to prepare yourself for the final confrontation with the Nephilim."

Malak raised his head proudly and met his master's dark eyes. "I am ready now," he proclaimed.

"Yes, I do believe you are." Verchiel motioned for him to rise. "But we must have patience. Soon enough it will be the heart of

Aaron Corbet that you have in your hand."
Verchiel gestured to the dripping heart the
hunter still held.

The hunter raised the angel heart in a toast to
his master. "This will be the Nephilim's heart,"
he said, bringing the bloody muscle to his
mouth and taking an enormous bite.

Verchiel nodded knowingly. "Far sooner
than you imagine."

Mr. Arslanian's voice had become nothing more
than a buzzing drone inside Vilma's head as she
nervously glanced at the tree outside the second-
story window. She flinched, for a moment expecting to see a man perched upon one of the
branches watching her. *I've got to stop this crazi-
ness,* she warned herself, trying to refocus on her
history teacher's lecture. She really had no idea
what the day's topic was, although she was certain it had something to do with the Civil War—
for when *didn't* a class of Mr. Arslanian's?

Vilma's eyes burned and she was sure they
were bloodshot and red, despite the drops she
constantly put in them. She needed sleep so
badly, just a few good hours, and then she was
sure she'd be good as new. But with sleep came
the dreams, and the visions of men perched in
the trees outside her bedroom windows. Images
from her nighttime terrors flashed through her
mind: fearsome angels, clad in golden armor,
destroying an ancient city; a girl, very much like

herself, fleeing through the desert as the creatures of Heaven pursued her; those same winged creatures descending upon the girl, dragging her up into the sky, ripping her apart, tearing the flesh from her—

"Miss Santiago?" beckoned a voice, and her entire body convulsed, sending her history book tumbling to the floor. The other students snickered, and she felt the warm flush of embarrassment spread across her face and down her neck. Vilma quickly retrieved her book from the floor, glancing to the front of the classroom where Judy Flannagan, the guidance office aide, was standing next to her teacher.

"Mrs. Beamis would like to see you," he said, looking annoyed.

"I'm sorry," she stammered as she gathered up her belongings and followed Judy from the room.

"It's okay," he responded, watching her go. "Didn't mean to startle you."

That also got a bit of a laugh from the class, adding a fresh bloom to her embarrassment as she closed the door behind her.

Book bag slung over her shoulder Vilma walked the now empty halls of Kenneth Curtis High School toward the guidance offices, wondering why Mrs. Beamis would want to see her now. She thought about the scholarship applications she'd completed over the past few months. *A little good news wouldn't hurt today*, she decided as she opened the door to the office and stepped into the small reception area.

Mrs. Vistorino, the office secretary, was busily working at her computer, clad in one of her usual pantsuits, this one a delicate powder blue. "Be with you in just a sec, hon." She finished her typing before tearing her attention away from the monitor. "What can I do for you, dear?" she asked, plucking her glasses from her face and letting them dangle from a gold chain around her neck.

"Mrs. Beamis wanted to see me?" Vilma said shyly, nervous anticipation beginning to grab hold of her.

"What's your name?" Mrs. Vistorino asked as she reached for the telephone next to her and pressed a button. Judy Flannagan came into the office behind her and gave her a polite smile before retrieving a stack of folders from Mrs. Vistorino's desk and going to a filing cabinet in the corner.

"Vilma Santiago," she answered, mesmerized by the simple act of the girl filing. *I need sleep—badly.*

"Vilma Santiago out here to see you," Mrs. Vistorino said into the receiver. There was a slight pause, and Vilma suddenly found herself praying for some kind of mistake. "Will do," the receptionist responded as she hung up the phone. "Go on in. Mrs. Beamis is waiting."

Vilma walked to the door and knocked

gently on the wooden frame. The counselor called out for her to enter, greeting her with a warm, friendly smile and motioning Vilma toward a chair in front of her desk. "Come in, Vilma," she said. "I'm sorry to pull you from class, but there's something I'd like to discuss with you and I'm afraid it couldn't wait."

Vilma lowered herself into the chair, taking the book bag from her shoulder and placing it on the floor beside her. "Nothing bad I hope," she said nervously. The office smelled of peppermint and she noticed that Mrs. Beamis had a piece of white-and-red-striped candy swishing around in her mouth as she studied an open file—hers, she imagined.

"No, nothing bad," she said, flipping through a few pages. "We're just a bit concerned right now." She looked up to meet Vilma's eyes.

Vilma's heart began to race. "What . . . what are you concerned about?"

The guidance counselor closed the folder and picked up a pen from the cluttered surface of her desk. "Since you transferred into Ken Curtis you've been one of our finest students, Vilma. Your teachers enjoy having you in their classes, and they say you're an excellent example for the other students. You're bright, articulate, and friendly; if we had a thousand more like you in this school, our jobs would be much easier."

Vilma found that she was blushing again. "Then why—"

"It's just that when a student such as your-self begins to act out of the ordinary, teachers notice, even students," she explained.

Vilma felt her heart sink. She had hoped she was hiding her problems well. But, evidently she was only fooling herself. It was having a far more noticeable effect on her than she'd thought.

"Is there anything you want to talk about?" Mrs. Beamis asked. "A problem here at school, or maybe even at home?"

The urge to confess rose in Vilma's throat. Maybe it would be for the best to talk about the dreams—about the bizarre things she thought she was seeing.

"We want to help you in any way we can, Vilma," the counselor continued. "There is no problem too big, you do understand that, don't you?"

She nodded as images of herself in a strait-jacket flashed through her mind. Mrs. Beamis would think she was crazy—and what if she was? What would she do then? "I've been very nervous about graduation," she lied. "About going off to college . . . It's been keeping me awake at night."

Mrs. Beamis tapped the pen tip on the cover of her folder. The woman's gaze was intense, as if she could see right through Vilma's ruse. "It is a very nerve-racking time of your life," she said, continuing to stare. "I can see where it might affect you."

Vilma laughed nervously. "It's just that I

know how much my life is going to change, and it scares me."

"Are you sure that's the only thing bothering you?" the counselor asked, moving forward in her chair.

Vilma slowly nodded as a creeping feeling of dread spread throughout her body. She thought of going to bed that night. She wanted to sleep so badly, but the dreams were so terrifying.

"No relationship issues?" Mrs. Beamis added. "We can talk about anything, Vilma. I can't stress that enough."

Vilma thought of Aaron Corbet. It had been more than a week since his last e-mail. His typed words—*I miss you, love, Aaron*—were like a knife blade to her chest. She had no idea where these feelings for a mysterious boy she barely knew had come from, but she found them almost as disturbing as her dreams.

"Nope." Vilma again shook her head. "No problems with boys."

She would have done just about anything to have Aaron back with her, for somehow she was certain that he could help with her problem. But that wasn't to be, and sometimes when she thought she would never see him again, it felt as though a part of her were dying.

"With everything I've had on my mind lately I really don't have the time for them."

The end-of-period bell started to ring and Vilma reached for her book bag leaning against the chair. "Is that all, Mrs. Beamis?" she asked, desperate to be out from beneath the microscope. "I've got a quiz in chemistry and I was hoping to review my—"

The guidance counselor picked up Vilma's file and placed it in a stack on the lefthand corner of her desk. "Yes, Vilma, I think we're finished here," she said with a caring smile.

Vilma returned the smile and stood. "Thanks for the talk and everything," she said, slinging the bag over her shoulder and turning to leave.

"Remember, no problem is too big," Mrs. Beamis called after her.

If only that were true, Vilma thought, waving good-bye to Mrs. Vistorino on her way to chemistry.

Deep down in the darkness, the power was angry.

As Aaron drifted in the void between oblivion and consciousness, he felt its indignation. He floated buoyantly within the ocean of black, the rage of the angelic charging the very atmosphere of the unconscious environment with its fearsome electricity, and then there came a tug and he was drawn upward toward awareness.

"I think he's waking up," he heard a familiar voice say as a wet tongue lapped his face, acting as a slimy lifeline to pull him farther from the depths of oblivion. Aaron opened his eyes and gazed up into Gabriel's looming face.

"There he is," the dog said happily. *"You've been out for quite some time. I was starting to get worried."*

Aaron reached up and scratched his canine friend behind one of his floppy, yellow ears. "Sorry about that, pal. Where's—"

"I'm here," Camael said from someplace nearby.

Aaron sat up and the world began to spin. "Damn," he said, touching a hand to his head. "Is everybody all right?"

"I'm hungry," Gabriel reported.

"You're always hungry," Aaron answered curtly. "What did she hit us with? Lightning?"

He noticed that his wrists were bound, encircled with manacles of golden metal, strange symbols scratched into their surface and a length of thick chain between them. There was a band of the same metal around his throat as well. "What the hell are these?" he asked, looking around.

It appeared that they were in the finished basement of a residential home. The Ping-Pong table, covered in what looked to be a couple of inches of dust and crammed into the far corner of the room, was a dead giveaway.

"The restraints were made by someone well versed in angel magick," Camael said from across the room. He was manacled as well and sitting stiffly in the center of a black beanbag chair. "The characters inscribed on them are powerful, imbuing the bonds with the capacity to render our abilities inert."

"No wonder my angel half is so ticked off," Aaron said, struggling to stand. "Is it common for fallen angels to keep prisoners in a rec room?" he asked. There was a mustiness in the air that hinted of dampness and decay. Dark patches of mildew grew on the cream-colored walls. There was also a strong smell of chemicals.

Gabriel plopped down in the warm patch where Aaron had been lying. The dog was famous for stealing space after it had been warmed up. He'd always hated having to get up during the night, only to return and find Gabriel curled up, pretending to be fast asleep in his spot.

"The fallen hide from their pursuers in all manner of places," Camael said, still awkwardly perched atop his beanbag chair. "Usually locales that have been lost to the world, hidden pockets forgotten or abandoned by the human thrall."

"Who are these guys, Camael?" he asked, walking toward carpeted steps that led up to a closed door. "They're not Powers, right?"

The angel warrior thought for a moment and then struggled to stand. It was the first time Aaron had seen Camael show anything but supreme agility and grace.

"Need a hand?" Aaron asked, moving toward the angel.

"I do not," Camael proclaimed, awkwardly rising to his feet. "These particular fallen could be from any number of the various clans that inhabit this world, perhaps a particular band that wishes to endear themselves to the Powers by handing us over to Verchiel," he said with a hint of foreboding.

"That would be very bad," Gabriel said from the floor, his snout nestled between his paws.

Aaron looked to the dog, but was distracted by the sound of the door opening above. He spun to face his captors as they slowly descended the stairs.

"Step away from the stairs, half-breed," said a low, rumbling voice with the slightest hint of a drawl. "I'd hate to put a bullet of fire in your brain before we had a chance to get acquainted and all."

Aaron heard a woman laugh and guessed it was the one who had brought the lightning down upon them. *Lorelei*, he remembered. *And . . . Lehash?*

He moved back and watched as the two they had confronted in the woods stepped into the basement, and this time they had brought someone else with them. The cowboy had his golden gun drawn, and it glowed in the semigloom. Aaron thought the sight particularly strange; he would never have thought of an angel looking this way. Actually he would never have imagined any of the angels he'd seen since his life had so dramatically changed, but an angelic gunslinger was certainly something he'd never considered.

Camael and Gabriel now stood with him before the mysterious trio. The other of the three, an angel like the cowboy, stepped toward them, meeting Aaron's gaze with an icy stare.

"Why have we been brought here?" Aaron asked, trying to stay civil.

The cowboy laughed, a toothpick moving from one side of his mouth to the other. "Tell 'em, Scholar."

"As designated constables, Lehash and Lorelei have taken it upon themselves to detain you so that we may determine whether you pose a threat to those citizens we have sworn to protect," the newest addition said rather formally.

He was dressed in a pristine white shirt and dark slacks and looked as though he should have been working in an accounting firm, instead of hanging with angels. *With guns*, Aaron reminded himself.

The cowboy angel, Lehash, plucked the toothpick from his mouth, his eyes upon them unwavering. "He does have a way with the words, don't he, Lorelei? If the citizens ever decide to elect a mayor, I'm gonna be the first to nominate Scholar here."

They both laughed, but the angel they called Scholar scowled.

"You keep talking about citizens," Aaron

said, still desperate to know what was going on. "Citizens of what? Where are we?"

Scholar was about to speak when Lehash cut him off. "Little piece a Heaven here on this god-forsaken ball of mud."

Lorelei nodded, smiling beautifully, and Aaron was struck by how attractive she really was. "Aerie," she said in the softest of whispers.

"Damn straight," Lehash said, placing the toothpick back in his mouth.

Aaron turned to Camael and saw an expression of shock register on the angel's face.

"After all this time," the angel warrior said, "I did not find it—it found me."

Can it be true?

Camael's mind raced. He gazed at the rather sordid surroundings, then back to his captors. He lurched toward them eagerly.

Lehash aimed his weapon, pulling back the hammer on the gun. "Not so fast there, chief," he growled.

Camael halted, his thoughts afire. He had to know more, he had to know if this was truly the oasis of peace for which he had been searching. "This is Aerie?" he asked breathlessly, a tiny part of him hoping that he had misunderstood.

"That's what we said," Lehash snarled, his aim unwavering. "Why? You've been looking for us?"

Camael nodded slowly, his sad gaze never leaving the three before him. Had Paradise also been tainted by the infection of violence? he wondered. Had he found what he most eagerly sought, only to see it in the throes of decay? "Far longer than any of you can possibly imagine."

"You were close," Scholar spoke up, his tone serious. "Most of your kind don't get this far. It's a good thing we caught you when we did."

"Our kind?" Aaron asked. "What's that supposed to mean?"

Lorelei shrugged, glaring at him defiantly. "Scholar was being nice. I would have called you what you really are—assassins, killers of dreams."

"They know what they are," Lehash said, the toothpick in his mouth sliding from one side to the other.

"You are mistaken," Camael said in an attempt to be the voice of reason. "The Powers soldiers that were slain attacked us. We were merely defending ourselves."

"Were you merely defending yourselves against the others as well?" Scholar asked.

Camael shook his head. "I don't understand—"

"*You* killed one of your own," Aaron blurted out, cutting him off. All eyes turned to the boy. "I watched you put a bullet in that guy's head back in the woods, and you're calling *us* assassins?" he asked incredulously. "You've got some nerve."

Camael sighed. It was sad that someone with

as much power as Aaron, was so lacking in diplomatic skills.

"That one wasn't much better than you," the girl said, a sneer upon her face.

"Was looking to sell the location of Aerie to whoever would give him the best deal," Lehash added.

"But you're probably aware of that already," Scholar finished.

Camael analyzed the situation. The beings before them believed that they were killers, probably working for Verchiel, and had come to destroy Aerie. He attempted to formulate a solution, but realized that the only way to convince the three that they meant no harm would be to explain about Aaron and his connection to the prophecy, although he seriously doubted they would even begin to believe that the boy—

"*Aaron is the One in the prophecy,*" he heard Gabriel suddenly say. The dog had strolled away from them and now sat patiently before their captors.

"Gabriel, get back here," Aaron commanded.

Lorelei squatted down in front of the dog meeting him eye to eye. She reached out and rubbed one of his ears. "Is that what you think?" she asked affectionately. "You must think your master is pretty special."

"Gabriel, come," the boy called to the Lab, but he did not respond.

"*I'm not the only one,*" he explained. "*Camael*

thinks so, and so does Verchiel. Do you have anything to eat? I'm hungry."

Lorelei rose slowly, eyeing Aaron as she did. "Is that what you think?" she asked, loathing in her voice.

Camael was silent, as was Aaron.

"Looks like we've got ourselves a celebrity," Lehash said with a grin that was absent of any humor whatsoever. "I say we finish this here and now before any more bull is slung." He drew another pistol of gold and aimed them both.

"No!" blurted out Scholar, as he reached over to push the weapons down. "We take them to the Founder and let him decide."

Gabriel turned to look at Aaron and Camael, his tail thumping happily on the concrete floor.

"We're going to see the Founder," he said. *"Maybe he'll have something for us to eat."*

chapter four

Belphegor pushed a wheelbarrow of dirt across the yard toward a row of blossoming rose bushes. A succession of summer rains had eroded some of the dirt at their base and he was eager to replace it before any of the plants' more delicate regions were exposed to the elements.

He set the barrow down, careful not to tip its contents, and picked up the shovel that was lying beside a rake in the sparse, brown grass. Belphegor plunged the shovel into the center of the mound of dirt and carried it to the rose-bushes, where he ladled it onto the ground beneath them. The wheelbarrow was nearly empty of its load before he felt that the bushes were properly protected.

The angel leaned upon his shovel and studied his work. The chemical pollutants that laced the rich, dark soil wafted up into the air, invisible to the human eye. With an angel's vision, however, Belphegor watched the poisonous particles drift heavily upon the summer breeze before settling back down to the tainted ground.

He squatted, digging his fingers into the newly shoveled dirt, and withdrew the contaminants, taking them into his own body. Belphegor shuddered and began to cough. There had been a time when purifying a stretch of land four times this area would have been nothing more than a trifle. But now, after so many years upon Earth and so much poison, it was beginning to have its effects upon him.

Is it worth it? he wondered, stepping back to admire the beauty he had helped create from the corrupted ground, beautiful red buds opening to the warmth of the sun. In his mind he pictured other gardens he had sown and knew that there was no question.

Belphegor picked up the metal rake and began to spread the new soil evenly about the base of the roses. In these gardens, left untended, he saw a reflection of himself and those who had chosen to join his community. Outcasts, each and every one, tainted in some way, desperately wanting to grow toward the sun—toward Heaven—but hindered by the poison that impaired them all.

He tried to force the sudden images away, but they had been with him for countless millennia and would likely remain with him for countless more. He remembered the poison that drove him from the kingdom of God to the world of man—the poison of indecision. The angel saw the war as if for the first time, no detail forgotten or fuzzy with the passage of time. His brethren locked in furious combat as he watched, lacking the courage within himself to take a side.

Belphegor stopped raking, forcing aside the painful remembrances to concentrate on the beauty he had helped to set free. Someday he hoped that he and all of Aerie's citizens would be as these roses: forgiven through penance and the fulfillment of an ancient prophecy, rising up out of the poisonous earth, reaching for the radiance of Heaven.

The sounds of voices, carried by the breeze, intruded on his thoughts, and reluctantly he turned from his roses to meet his visitors. He walked through the expanse of yard, and around to the front of the abandoned dwelling, its windows boarded up and covered with spray-painted graffiti. It had once been the home of a family of six, with hopes and dreams very much like many of the other families that had lived within the Ravenschild housing development. Belphegor could still feel their sadness radiating from the structures in the desolate neighborhood, the echoes of life silenced by a corporation's greedy little secret. The ChemCord chemical company had buried its waste here, poisoning the land and those who lived in homes built upon it. It was a sad place, this

Ravenschild housing development, but it was now *their* home, the latest Aerie for those who awaited forgiveness.

Belphegor glanced down the sidewalk to see his constables approaching with two others— and a dog. *These must be the ones suspected of murder*, he thought, recalling the sudden, violent increase in deaths of fallen angels scattered about the world. He would question these strangers, but he had already decided their fate. Earth was a dangerous place for the likes of the fallen, and he would do anything to keep his people and their community safe. With that in mind, he steeled himself to pass judgment, studying the captives as they approached.

Belphegor gasped as he suddenly realized that one of the strangers was not that at all. He knew the angel that walked with the boy. They had been friends once, before the war, before his own fall from grace.

"Camael," Belphegor whispered, his thoughts drifting to the last time he had seen his heavenly brother. "Have you finally come to finish what you failed to do so very long ago?"

the garden of eden, soon after the great war

Camael drew back his arm and brought down his sword of fire with the same devastating results as during the heavenly conflict. The impossibly thick wall of vegetation that had grown between the gates of Paradise was no match for his blazing weapon, the seemingly impenetrable barrier of tangled plant life parting with the descent of his lethal blade. It had not been long since the eviction of humans from the Garden, yet already the once perfect habitat for God's newest creations was falling prey to ruin.

Animals from every genus fled before him, sensing the murderous purpose that had brought him to this place. The war had finally been won by the armies of the Lord and the defeated—the legions of the Morningstar—had been driven from Heaven. As leader of the Powers host, it had fallen to him to track and destroy those who opposed the Almighty and brought the blight of war to the most sacred of places.

Camael had come to the Garden in search of one such criminal, one that had once served the glory of the Creator as devoutly as he—but that had been before the war, and things were no longer as they once were. Belphegor would pay for his crimes, as would all who took up arms against the Lord of Lords.

Camael stopped before another obstruction of root, tree, and vine, and with his patience on the wane, slashed out with his fiery blade, venting some of the rage that had been his constant companion since the war began. His fury poured forth in torrents as his sword cut a swath of flaming devastation through the Garden of

Paradise, his roar of indignation mixing with the cries of panicked animals.

How could they have done this to the Lord God—the Creator of all there is? His thoughts raged as he lashed out at the thick vegetation, the vestiges of battles he had so recently fought still raw and bleeding upon his mind. His anger spent, Paradise burned around him and the barriers of growth fell away to smoldering ash. Camael beheld a clearing, void of life except for a single tree—and the one he was searching for.

Belphegor stood before what could only have been the Tree of Knowledge—large with golden bark, and carrying sparsely among its canopy of yellow leaves, a forbidden fruit that shone like a newly born star in the night sky.

"Belphegor," Camael said, stepping through the burning brush and into the clearing. In his hand he still clutched his weapon of fire, and it sparked and licked at the air, eager to be used.

Hand pressed to the tree's body, the angel Belphegor turned to glance at him and smiled sadly. "It's dying," he said, returning his attention to the tree. "And it will be only a matter of time before what is killing it spreads to the remainder of the Garden."

Camael stopped and glared at his fallen brethren. His anger, though abated by the destructive tantrum, still thrummed inside.

"It's His disappointment," Belphegor said,

again looking at Camael. "The Creator's disappointment in the man and woman—it's acting as a poison, gradually killing everything that He made especially for them. I'm doing my best to slow the process, but I'm afraid it's only a matter of time before it is all lost."

Camael gripped his sword tighter and spoke the words that had been trapped in his throat. They spilled from his mouth, reeking of anger and despair. "I've come to kill you, Belphegor." He wasn't sure how he expected the fallen angel to react—perhaps to cower with fear, or suddenly flee deeper into the Garden—but it appeared that Belphegor had already accepted his lot.

"I'm glad it's you who has come for me," he said casually, moving away from the tree toward Camael.

Camael pointed his sword, halting the angelic fugitive's progress.

Belphegor stared at him over the sputtering blade of fire. "If it is time for me to die, then I accept my fate."

The Powers' commander seethed. *How dare such a sinner surrender without a fight. How dare he deny me the wrath of battle.* "You will summon a weapon and fight me," he snarled.

Belphegor slowly shook his head. "I did not fight in the war and I will not fight you, my friend," he said sadly. "If you are to take my life, do it now, for I am ready."

Camael wanted to strike the angel down, lift his fearsome blade above his head and cleave the traitor in two, but something stayed his hand—the question that had plagued his tortured thoughts since the war began. "Why, Belphegor?" he asked, his body trembling with repressed anger.

The fallen angel sighed and sat down in the shade of the Tree of Knowledge. Camael loomed above him, his blade of fire poised for attack.

"I did not want to fight," Belphegor said, picking up a dry stalk of grass and twirling it between his fingers. "For either side."

"He is your Creator, Belphegor," Camael spat. "How could you not fight for Him?"

The fallen angel turned his gaze up to Camael and the look upon his face was one of resignation. "I could not even begin to think of raising a weapon against my brothers—or my Creator. If that makes me an enemy of Heaven, so be it."

"It makes you a coward," Camael said, tightening his grip upon his weapon's hilt.

"Is that really how you feel, Camael?" Belphegor asked without a hint of fear. "Have you come for me not because of what *I* did not do—but for what *you* did not have the courage to do yourself?"

The words were like a savage attack, weapons of truth hacking away at Camael to reveal the painful reality. There had been so much death, and he could see no end to it.

Camael swung his blade and buried it mere inches from Belphegor. The ground around the weapon began to burn.

"Damn you," he hissed, pulling the sword from the smoldering earth and stepping back, his steely stare still upon his foe. In his mind's eye he saw them, the faces of all he had slain in the battle for Heaven, a seemingly endless parade of death marching through his memories, and it chilled him to his core. Once they had been like him, serving the one true God—and then came dissension, sides were chosen and a war begun.

"You must be made to answer for your crimes," he said as Belphegor rose to his feet.

"Haven't we been punished enough?" the fallen angel asked. "Rejected, forced to abandon all we have ever known to live amongst animals—most, I think, already suffer a fate far worse than what awaits at your hands." Belphegor moved closer. "Death at your hands might even be considered an act of mercy."

Camael placed the tip of his sword beneath Belphegor's throat and the flesh there bubbled and burned—yet despite this, the fallen angel did not pull away.

"We were brothers once," Camael whispered, staring at Belphegor's face twisted in pain. "But no more," he said as he pulled the blade away. "It will be as if you were destroyed by my hand."

Belphegor gingerly touched the charred and oozing flesh beneath his chin. "Will this mercy be bestowed upon the others as well?" he asked, his voice a gentle whisper.

Camael turned and prepared to leave Eden.

"How many more will have to die?" Belphegor called after him as Camael reached the edge of the clearing. "When will it be enough, Camael?" the fallen angel asked. "And when will we finally be allowed to show our sorrow for what we have done?"

Camael left the Garden of Eden, never to look upon it again, Belphegor's questions reverberating through his mind. He did not respond to his fallen brother, for he did not have the answers, and he had begun to wonder if ever he truly would.

aerie, present day

The sight of Belphegor stirred memories Camael had not experienced for millennia. Pictures of the past billowed and whirled, like desert sands agitated by the winds of storm. The angel warrior quickly suppressed them.

"Hello, Camael," Belphegor said, standing on the sidewalk in front of a boarded-up home. "It's been quite some time."

Camael looked closely at the fallen angel before him; he appeared old, almost sickly. It was common for angels that had fled to Earth to allow themselves to age, to fit in with their new environment, but Belphegor's look was more than that.

"I executed you," Camael said, remembering the day he had stormed from the Garden of Eden without completing his assignment.

"Is that what you told your Powers' comrades—did you actually tell them that I died at your hand?"

Camael recalled addressing his troops before their journey to Earth. He remembered telling them, the lie already beginning to eat at him, the doubts about their mission, seeded by Belphegor, already starting to sprout. "I was their leader, they would believe anything I told them."

"And now?" Belphegor asked.

"Now they would like to see me as dead as they believe you to be."

The old angel studied Camael's face, obviously searching for signs of untruth. "I had heard that you left them, but was still saddened that it took as long as it did."

"It was when I read the words of the prophecy that I realized it wasn't the way," Camael answered. "There had already been too much death. I began to believe that a new future for our kind rests in the hands of a half-breed—a Nephilim, chosen by God."

Camael looked at Aaron, who shifted his feet nervously at the attention now placed upon him.

"That would be me, I guess," he said.

The constables, who had been silent until that point, chuckled at the idea of this Nephilim boy being the Chosen One, but Camael waited to see how Belphegor would respond.

"You believe this one to be the Chosen?" he asked, pointing at Aaron with a long gnarled finger.

Camael noticed the dirt beneath his nails. "Yes, I believe it is so," he answered.

"Have you ever heard anything so foolish, Belphegor?" Lehash asked, scratching the side of his grizzled face with the golden barrel of his gun. "Next they'll be telling us that they ain't had nothin' to do with the rash a' killin's this last week."

Silently Belphegor moved closer to Aaron. "Are you?" he asked as he began to sniff him from head to toe.

"I have no idea what they're talking about," Aaron explained. "We tried to tell them that before, but—"

"There's quite a bit of violence locked up inside you," Belphegor said, stepping back and wiping his nose with a finger. "Powerful stuff, wild—wouldn't take much, I imagine, to set you on a killing spree."

Camael stepped forward to defend the boy. "Aaron has accomplished much since the angelic nature has awakened. I've seen him use his power, on more than one occasion, to send a fallen angel home."

Belphegor tilted his head to one side. "Home?" he questioned, deep crow's feet forming at the corners of his squinting eyes. "What do you mean?"

Camael nodded slowly, allowing the meaning of his words to sink in. "*Home,*" he said, still nodding. "He sent them home to Heaven."

Lehash began to laugh uproariously, looking to his fellow constables to join him. They smiled uneasily. Camael scowled, he did not care to have his motivations questioned and would have given everything to be free of the magickally augmented manacles.

The constable strode forward, puffing out his chest. "Go ahead, boy," he said, holding his arms out. "I'm ready. Send me home to God."

"It . . . it doesn't work that way," Aaron stammered. "I just can't do it—something inside tells me when it's time."

Lehash laughed again, as if he'd never heard anything as funny, and Camael seethed.

"Silence, Lehash," Belphegor ordered again, scrutinizing Aaron. "Is that true, boy?" he asked. "Have you sent fallen angels back to Heaven?"

Gabriel, who had been unusually quiet, suddenly padded toward Belphegor. "*I saw him do it,*" the dog said in all earnest. "*And he made me better after I was hurt. Do you have anything to eat? I'm very hungry.*"

Belphegor studied the animal, whose tail

wagged eagerly. "This animal has been altered," he said, looking first to Camael, and then to Aaron. "Who would do such a thing?"

"He was hurt very badly," Aaron explained. "I . . . I didn't even know what I was doing. I talked to the thing living inside me. . . . I begged it to save Gabriel and—"

Belphegor raised a hand to silence Aaron. "I've heard enough," he said. "The idea of such power in the hands of someone like you chills me to the bone."

"What should we do with them?" Lehash asked. There was a cruel look in his eyes, and Camael was convinced that he would do whatever Belphegor told him, no matter how dire.

"Take them back to the house," the old angel said, turning toward the fenced yard he had come from. "I need time to think."

"Listen to me, Belphegor," Camael again tried to explain. "No matter how wrong it may seem to you, Aaron *is* the one you've been waiting for. Even the Archangel Gabriel believed it to be so. You have to trust me on this."

The fallen angel returned his attention to Camael. "God's most holy messenger is not here to vouch for him, and I'm afraid trust is in very short supply here these days," Belphegor said sadly. "There's far too much at stake. I'm sorry." He looked to his people. "Take them back to the house, and be sure to keep the restraints on them."

Lehash grabbed hold of Aaron, but the boy fought against him.

"Listen," he cried out, and Belphegor stopped to stare at the Nephilim. "I'm trying to find my little brother—he's the only real family I have left."

Belphegor looked away, seemingly uninterested in the boy's plight.

"Please!" he yelled. "Verchiel has him and I have to get him back. Let us go, and we'll leave you alone, we promise."

The old fallen angel ignored the boy, continuing on his way. Lehash again gripped him by the arm and pulled. "C'mon, boy. He don't want to hear any more of your nonsense."

"Goddam it!" Aaron shouted. "If you're not going to listen, I'll *make* you listen!"

And then he did something he should not have been able to do with the magickal restraints in place.

Aaron Corbet began to change.

chapter five

Aaron knew that time was of the essence and felt his patience stretched to its limits. The fallen angels, these citizens of Aerie, weren't listening to him. He didn't have time to be locked away in the playroom of some abandoned house. The Powers had Stevie, and the thought of his little brother still in the clutches of the murderous Verchiel acted like a key to unleash the power within him. Before he realized what he was doing, anger and guilt had unlocked the cage door, inviting the wild thing out to play. Aaron felt his transformation begin, and this time it hurt more than anything he could remember.

He turned to glare at Lehash, who still held his arm. "Let go of me," he snarled, and felt a certain amount of satisfaction when the fallen angel did as he was told.

The pain was incredible, and Aaron could

only guess it was because of the magickal restraints he still wore on his wrists and around his neck. He could feel the sigils burning upward from beneath his skin to decorate his flesh. They felt like small rodents with sharp, nasty claws, frantically digging to the surface. He screamed as sparks jumped from the golden manacles. The power within him wasn't about to back down, even if it killed him.

He found Belphegor's wide-eyed stare and held it with eyes as black as night. "Look at me!" Aaron cried. "Can't you see that we're telling the truth?"

He lurched toward the ancient fallen angel, crackling arcs of supernatural energy streaming from the enchanted restraints. From behind him he heard Camael and Gabriel call out for him to stop—but he couldn't. He had to make Belphegor realize that they meant the people of Aerie no harm.

The constables were beside him. Lehash was aiming his guns, pulling back the golden hammers, while Lorelei had raised her hands and was mumbling something that sounded incredibly old. The one called Scholar stood at Belphegor's side, ready to defend the wizened fallen angel if necessary.

"Give me the word, boss," Lehash sneered, "and I'll drop him where he stands."

"No!" Belphegor ordered, raising his hand.

The sigils had finally burned their way to the

surface of Aaron's flesh, but there was no relief from the pain. His wings of ebony black had begun to expand on his back, but were hindered by the magick within the sparking bonds. The pain was just too much, and he fell to his knees upon the desiccated lawn in front of the abandoned home. "You've got to listen," he moaned.

"Could just any Nephilim override the magicks of the manacles, Belphegor?" he heard Camael ask above the roar of anguish deafening his ears.

"He is powerful, I'll grant him that," Belphegor replied. "But I've met powerful halflings in my time, and that doesn't make them prophets. Matter of fact, most are dead now, driven insane by power they couldn't begin to understand, never mind tame."

"And the markings?" Camael asked. "What do you make of them?"

Aaron opened his eyes to see the leader of Aerie kneeling beside him with Scholar. "I want to know what they mean," Belphegor said, gesturing to the archaic symbols decorating the Nephilim's face and arms. Scholar removed a pad of paper and pen from his back pocket and began to copy them.

"Do you believe me now?" Aaron asked weakly, exhausted from the battle between the angelic force and the magick within the golden restraints.

Belphegor stared at him with eyes ancient

and inhuman, and he felt like some kind of new germ beneath a scientist's microscope. "The question is, boy, do *you* believe that you are the Chosen?" Belphegor asked.

Aaron wanted to tell him what he wanted to hear, what would allow them their freedom, but he couldn't. Although Camael and even the Archangel Gabriel believed he was the savior, the truth was, Aaron still saw himself as just a kid from Lynn, Massachusetts. Certainly he couldn't deny his power, but did that make him the Chosen One?

I just don't know.

"I . . . I'm not sure," he told Belphegor, and felt the power begin to recede.

The old angel smiled and rose to his feet.

"Should we take them back to the house?" Lorelei asked. She had moved up behind the older angel, and Aaron noticed that her fingertips still crackled with the residual of her unused spell.

"I don't think that will be necessary," Belphegor replied. "Let them have the run of the place, but the manacles stay on until I'm sure they can be trusted."

"Are you out of your mind, old man?" Lehash asked. The others looked uncomfortable with his outburst. "With so much going on out there, you're gonna give them free reign? They'll be murderin' us in our sleep before—"

"You heard me, Lehash," Belphegor said as

he turned his back and strode through the yard. "Welcome to Aerie, folks," he said, and disappeared around the corner of the abandoned house.

The prisoner's eyes opened with a sound very much like late fall leaves crackling underfoot, head bent and gazing down upon hands charred and blackened. He was sitting up against the bars of his cage, his entire body enveloped in a cocoon of sheer agony. His fingers slowly straightened, and through scorched and bleary eyes, he watched as flakes of burnt flesh rained on his lap.

He wasn't positive when Verchiel had left, but he was glad to see the Powers' leader gone, for as bored as he was, imprisoned within the cage, he did not care for the angel's company in the least. *High maintenance that one,* he thought, shifting his position in an attempt to get comfortable and accomplishing nothing more than additional waves of excruciating pain. *Very temperamental.*

The smell of overcooked meat wafted about the inside of the cage and the prisoner was reminded of a feast he had attended in a Serbian village not long before taking up residence in the Crna Reka Monastery. They had been celebrating the birth of a child, and had cooked a pig on a spit over a roaring fire. They had welcomed him to their celebration; a total stranger invited to partake of their happiness. So he did, and for a brief moment was able to forget all that he was, and the horrors for which he was responsible. Moments like that were few and far between in his interminable existence, and he held onto each like the most precious of jewels.

From the corner of his eye he spied movement, a tiny, dark shape scurrying along the wall toward the hanging cage. His friend the mouse had returned. The prisoner leaned back to see outside the cage, and some skin from his neck sloughed off between the bars to sprinkle the floor like black confetti. The air felt cool against his exposed flesh. He was healing, despite the hindering magicks in the metal of the cage.

"Hello," he croaked, his voice little more than a dry whisper.

The mouse responded with a succession of tiny squeaks.

"I'm fine," the prisoner answered. He leaned over until he was lying on his side and extended a blackened arm through the bars of the cage. The mouse began to squeak again, and he was touched by the tiny creature's concern.

"Don't worry about me," he told the mouse. "Pain and I have a very unique relationship."

The animal then sprung from the floor to land on the prisoner's upturned hand and scrambled up the length of his arm into the cage.

"That's it," he cooed, still lying on his side, the mouse squatting before his face, nose, and whiskers twitching curiously.

"I'll be fine, little one. A bit more time and I'll be good as new."

The mouse squeaked once and then again, tilting its head as it studied his condition.

"Yes, it hurts a great deal. But that's all part of the game. It's not as if I don't deserve every teeth-gritting twitch of pain."

The mouse squeaked, moving closer to his face. It nuzzled affectionately against the burned skin on his nose, gently rubbing it away to expose new flesh, pink and raw.

"No," the prisoner said. "You just *think* I'm a good man; you didn't know me before."

Memories of times he'd rather have forgotten danced past the theater of his mind, and the prisoner struggled to right himself. His furry companion dug its claws into his shoulder and held on as he braced himself against the bars of the cage.

"What kind of man was I before? Do you really want to know?" he asked with a dry chuckle. The mouse began to clean itself, comfortably perched upon the prisoner's shoulder.

"That's a good idea," he told his friend. "You're going to feel pretty dirty when I'm done."

The pain was no worse, and neither was it better, but this was old hat for him. He was a pro when it came to pain. It was always with him, whether his flesh was burned and blackened or he was sleeping peacefully on a woven mat in a Serbian monastery. It was his punishment, and he deserved it.

"You've got to promise that once you hear my story, you won't leave me for some other fallen angel."

The mouse gave him an encouraging squeak, and the prisoner's breath rattled in his seared, fluid-filled lungs as he took a deep breath.

"It all started in Heaven," he began, and the depth of his sorrow streamed from his mouth like blood from a mortal wound.

"So, where are all these citizens you guys keep talking about?" Aaron asked as they walked down the cracked and uneven sidewalk past one lifeless house after another.

"They're around," Lorelei answered with a flip of her snow-white locks. "After the business with that Johiel creep, I don't think they're too eager to roll out the red carpet for anybody new. I can't believe he was going to sell us out just to save his own butt." She shook her head in disgust as she crossed the street at a crosswalk. "Can't trust anyone these days," she said with a warning glance over her shoulder.

"How long has it been here?" Camael asked, scrutinizing the neighborhood with eyes more perceptive than a hawk's.

"What?" the girl asked. "Aerie? I've been here six years, and this is the only place I've ever known. Although I hear it's been in lots of different places: on the side of an active volcano, in an abandoned coal mine . . . one of the old-timers said he lived inside a sunken cruise ship at the bottom of the Atlantic Ocean. Aerie seems to be wherever the citizens are."

Camael nodded slowly. "That is why it was so difficult to find," he said, his eyes still taking it all in. "It does not stay in one location."

Gabriel was sniffing around the weather-beaten front steps of one of the abandoned homes; he sounded like the clicks of a Geiger counter searching for radiation. On a house in front of them, a large piece of plywood had been nailed across the entryway where the front door should have been. Crudely spray-painted on the wood were the words MY FAMILY DIED FOR LIVING HERE.

"What happened here?" Aaron asked, the message affecting him far more than he would have imagined. It was as if he could feel the grief streaming from each of the painted words as thoughts of his foster parents, their horrible demise, and his own home destroyed by flames flashed through his mind.

Lorelei stopped and looked at the house with him. "During the 1940s and 1950s this property was owned by ChemCord. They were producers of industrial pesticides, acids, organic solvents, and whatnot, and they used to dump their waste here." She pointed to the street beneath her feet.

"The place stinks, Aaron," Gabriel said as he relieved himself on the withered, brown remains of a bush in front of the house. *"The dirt smells bad—like poison."*

"And that's helping?" he asked the dog.

"Can't hurt it," Gabriel responded haughtily, and continued his exploration.

"He's right, really," Lorelei said. "They dumped excess chemicals and by-products in metal drums that they buried all over this property; tons and tons of the stuff."

They continued to walk, each home taking on new meaning for Aaron. "Then how could they build houses—an entire neighborhood—here?" he asked.

"ChemCord went belly up in 1975 and they began to sell off their assets—including undeveloped land. As far as the guys at ChemCord were concerned, the property was perfectly safe."

"There is much sadness here," Camael said from behind them. They turned to see that he was staring at another of the homes. A rusted tricycle lay on its side in front, a kind of marker for the sorrow that emanated from each of the homes. "It has saturated these structures; I can see why Belphegor and the others would be drawn to it."

"So let me guess," Aaron began. "They built on the land and people started to get sick."

Lorelei nodded. "They started construction of Ravenschild Estates in 1978, and the families began to move in during the spring of 1980. Everything was perfect bliss, until the first case of leukemia and then the second, and the third, and then came the birth defects."

"How many people died?" Aaron asked. The wind blew down the deserted street kicking up dust, and he could have sworn he heard the faint cries of the mournful in the breeze.

"I'm really not sure," the woman answered. "I know a lot of kids got sick before the state got involved in 1989. They investigated and forced the families to evacuate. They ended up purchasing more than three hundred and fifty homes and financing some of the relocation costs."

"So it's kind of like a ghost town," Aaron said, still listening to the haunted cries upon the wind.

"Yeah, it is," Lorelei answered.

"What did your friend Lehash call this place?" he asked, his nose wrinkled with displeasure. "A little piece of paradise? I'm not seeing that at all."

Lorelei looked about, a dreamy expression on her pale, attractive features. "It may not look like much," she said quietly, "but it's lots better than what I left behind. I'll take this over the nuthouse any day of the week." She abruptly turned and continued on her way.

Her words piqued Aaron's curiosity, and he

sped up to walk beside her. "Did you say you were in a nuthouse?"

Lorelei didn't answer right away, as if she were deciding whether or not she wanted to talk about it. "A pretty good one too—or so I've been told," she finally said. "I was seventeen, on the verge of my eighteenth birthday, and everything I'd ever known turned to shit."

Aaron could hear the pain in her voice and immediately sympathized. He understood exactly what she was talking about. "It was the . . . the power inside you . . . the whole Nephilim thing."

She nodded. "I didn't know it then, but I finally figured it out after one of my last hospital stays. I was on the streets and had stopped taking my medications and things started to become clearer. 'Course that's what crazy people not taking their medicines always say." She laughed, but it was a laugh filled with bitterness.

Aaron suddenly saw in the young woman a kindred spirit and wondered if her story would have been his if not for the whole prophecy thing.

"I was drawn to this place," Lorelei continued. "As the drugs that I'd been pumped full of left my system I could feel the pull of Aerie—I was seeing it in my dreams, along with all kinds of other nonsense that I'm sure you're familiar with."

"Were there those that attempted to harm you?" Camael chimed in, making reference to the Powers. "Trying to keep you from reaching this destination?"

A lock of white hair drifted in front of her face, and she swept it away with the back of her hand. "I got really good at avoiding them." She turned to the angel. "At first I thought they were just manifestations of my paranoid delusions, but when one tried to burn me alive inside an old tenement house I was crashing in, I realized that wasn't the case."

"You were lucky to have survived."

Lorelei agreed. "I think that the power inside was helping me. Without the drugs, it was growing and helping me to find a place where I could be safe."

They passed an enormous mound of burned and blackened wood that had been piled in the center of the street. Aaron could see that some doors and windows, railings and banisters from some of the houses had made it onto the stack. He looked from the charred pyre to her.

"We had problems with some local kids," she explained. "Liked to use the place to party. We were afraid their little bonfires would eventually burn it down."

"What did you do?" Aaron asked.

Lorelei extended her hands and small sparks of radiant energy danced from one fingertip to the next. "After I finally got here and realized I wasn't crazy, that I was Nephilim, I learned that I had an affinity for angel magick. My father and I did some spells to scare the kids away. This place has a real reputation now, even worse than it had before."

"Your father? Who? . . ."

"Lehash," she answered. "Pretty cool, huh? Not only was I not insane, but I hooked up with my dad the angel, and suddenly everything began to make a weird kind of sense."

The words of the Archangel Gabriel echoed through Aaron's mind—*You have your father's eyes*—and Aaron wondered if the mystery of his own parentage would ever be revealed to him.

On a tiny side street they stopped in front of a house with powder blue aluminum siding, strings of Christmas lights still dangling from the gutters.

"Is that my car?" Aaron asked, moving past Lorelei toward the vehicle parked in front.

Gabriel beat him there and gave the vehicle the once over. *"It's our car, Aaron,"* he said, tail wagging. *"I can smell our stuff."*

"One of the citizens retrieved it from the Burger King parking lot." Lorelei gestured toward the house. "This is where you'll be staying."

Aaron gave the house another look and felt his aggravation level rise. He didn't want to stay; he wanted to continue the search for his brother. They had done nothing wrong, and Belphegor had no right to keep them here. "How long are you planning to hold us?" he asked, staring down in growing anger at the manacles fastened around his wrist. "If I'm ever going to find my brother—"

"You'll stay as long as the Founder says you'll stay," Lorelei interrupted, crossing her arms in defiance. "As far as we're concerned, you're the ones responsible for all the killings. And, until we know otherwise, you're not going anywhere."

"That's crap and you know it," he growled, the angelic presence perking up within him. It would never miss an opportunity for conflict and he had to steel himself against the urge to let it free. He had no desire to feel the effects of the manacles' magicks again.

"If my father had his way," she interjected, "you'd still be locked in that basement, Chosen One or otherwise." Lorelei took a step closer, fists clenched by her side. "What makes you think you're so damn special anyway?" she demanded.

"I didn't ask for this!" Aaron pushed past the woman, heading in the opposite direction.

"Where are you going?"

He stopped, but didn't turn around. "I need to take a walk. Besides, Gabriel is hungry and I wouldn't mind a bite to eat myself. Is there any-place around here where we can get some food?"

Lorelei didn't answer right away, as if she were considering not letting him go. Aaron decided that would be a very bad idea on her part, for his angelic nature was already coiled and ready to strike. Looking for trouble.

"You're heading in the right direction," she finally said. "Take a left onto Gagnon. You'll see the community center at the end of the street. Should be able to get a sandwich or something there."

"Thanks," he said, starting to walk again. Gabriel followed close at his side, but Camael remained with Lorelei. "I'll see you guys later."

"Yeah," Lorelei called after him. "You will, and as soon as you get used to the idea, things'll be a little easier for you."

Marshall County Public Library
1003 Poplar Street
Benton, KY 42025

chapter six

Camael watched Aaron leave and could not help but share some of the Nephilim's discontent.

"So, what do you *really* think?" Lorelei asked as they stood on the sidewalk before the shabby house. "Do you seriously believe that he's the Chosen One?"

He turned away from the boy and his dog walking off in the distance and met her gaze. "I believe there is something special about that one," he answered.

"I had a cat when I was eight that was pretty special, but it doesn't mean that she was the Messiah." Lorelei's tone dripped sarcasm.

Camael chose to ignore her jibes and instead addressed the dwelling before them. "This is where we will be staying then?" he asked, as if in need of clarification.

"This is it," she answered. "One of the sturdier homes, no leaks and still unchristened by local youths brave enough to come here."

"It will do," he said, and then was quiet. He hoped that his silence would act as a dismissal to the female half-breed. The angel did not feel like talking; there was much he needed to reflect upon, and he found her presence distracting.

"You didn't answer my question," the Nephilim piped up, eager to press the sensitive issue. "Do you believe he's the One in the prophecy?"

"It matters not what I believe," he said, his pale blue eyes locked on hers, "for it appears you and yours have already made up your minds about the boy."

"We've seen a lot of so-called prophets here. Hell, I've seen at least two since I've been around. It takes more than the word of a former Powers' commander to convince us," she answered, arms folded across her chest. "Sorry to doubt you, but that's just the way it is."

He could sense that she wanted more, that she wanted him to convince her he was right. But as he stood on the desolate street, in the abandoned neighborhood that he had come to learn was the paradise he'd sought for centuries, Camael found that he just didn't have the strength.

"I have searched for this place far longer than even I can recall," he said, gesturing to the homes and the neighborhood around him. "If it is permitted, I would like to explore Aerie on my own."

Lorelei nodded slightly. There was disappointment in her look, and for that he was truly sorry. "Sure, it's permitted, knock yourself out." She placed her hands inside the pockets of her short jacket. "The manacles and choke collar should keep you out of trouble." She turned on her heel and crossed the street to leave him alone.

"It ain't much," he heard the Nephilim say as she slowly headed back in the direction they had come. "But it's home."

Camael wasn't sure what he had expected of Aerie but was certain, as he strolled down the deathly silent street with its houses in sad disrepair and the offensive aroma of chemical poisoning tainting the air, that this was not even remotely what he had imagined it would be.

What did you think you would find? he silently asked, the setting sun at his back. *An earthly version of a Heaven lost so long ago? Is that it?* he wondered. Was that why he was feeling so out of sorts?

In the distance before him, the angel could see the golden cross atop the steeple of a church, and found himself pulled to this human place of worship. Its architecture was far more contemporary than he cared for—simple, less ornate than many of the other places of worship he had visited in his long years upon the planet of man. Slowly he climbed the weathered concrete steps of the structure, feeling the residue of prayer left by the devout. He pulled open the door, and traces of the love these often primitive creatures felt for their Creator cascaded over him in waves.

Camael stepped inside the church, letting the door slowly close behind him. The structure had been stripped of its religious trappings; nowhere was there a crucifix or relic of a saint to be found. He guessed that such religious paraphernalia had been removed when the church was abandoned, but that did not change the feeling of the place. This was a place for worship, and no matter what iconic trappings had been taken from it, it could not change its original purpose.

Crudely constructed benches were lined up before the altar at the front of the building and Camael saw that he was not alone. A man, a Nephilim, sat at the front, his gaze intent upon an image that had been painted on the cream-colored wall at the back of the altar.

Camael walked closer. The artwork was crudely rendered, but there was no mistaking what it depicted—the joining of mortal woman and angel. A child hung in the air above its mismatched parents on wings of holy light, its tiny arms spread wide, the rays of light that haloed its head spreading upward to God, as well as drenching the world below them in its divine illumination. He found himself studying the artist's rendition of the child, searching for any similarity with his own charge, the boy Aaron Corbet. Of course there were none, and he felt foolish for looking.

The lone figure sitting before the altar turned with a start, his face contorting in wide-eyed astonishment as his gaze fell upon Camael. The angel considered speaking to the halfling, but before he could put the words together, the man leaped from his seat and fled through a nearby exit.

These citizens certainly don't trust strangers, Camael thought as he strode to the front of the old church and sat on the bench the Nephilim had vacated. The silence was comforting, and he closed his eyes, losing himself deep within his thoughts. It was not often that he had a chance to reflect.

He thought of the war in Heaven. It had seemed so black and white at the beginning: Those who opposed the Lord of Lords would be punished, it was as simple as that. Faces appeared before his eyes, brothers of the myriad heavenly hosts; some had been with him since their inception, but it mattered not, for they had to pay the price. And then it was too much for him, the smell of their blood choking his breath, their screams for mercy deafening his ears. There seemed to be no end, his existence had become one of vengeance and misery. He had become a messenger of death and he could stand it no more. *And then there was the prophecy. . . .*

Camael opened his eyes to look upon the image painted on the wall before him: the strange trinity that would herald the end of so much pain and suffering. He remembered when he had first heard the prophecy told by a human seer. He desperately wanted it to be true, for God's forgiveness to be bestowed upon those who had fallen, by a being that was an amalgam of His most precious creations.

From that moment, Camael had looked upon these creatures—these Nephilim—as conduits of God's mercy, and he did everything in his power to keep them safe. These times had been long and filled with violence, but also salvation. He had taken it upon himself to find the Nephilim of prophecy, to help bring about the redemption of his fallen brethren, and at last it had brought him here.

To Aerie.

The angel looked around at the sparse environment in which he sat, and was overcome with feelings of disappointment. *Is this to be where the Lord's mercy is finally realized? A human neighborhood built upon a burial ground of toxic waste.* Camael was loath to admit it, but he was expecting more.

Even though lost in thought, he sensed their presence and rose from his seat to see that he

was no longer alone. The Nephilim that had fled
the church when he'd first arrived had returned,
and brought others with him. They streamed
into the place of worship, male and female of
various ages—all of them the result of the joining of human and angel. They whispered and
muttered among themselves as they stared at
Camael.

He had no idea what they wanted of him
and on reflex tried to conjure a sword of fire. But
the magick that infused the manacles encircling
his wrists and throat immediately kicked in. The
angel shrieked in pain as daggers of ice plunged
through his body. He fell to his knees, cursing
his stupidity, and struggled to stay conscious as
the waves of discomfort gradually abated.

The throng of Nephilim came at him then,
and there was nothing he could do to stop them.
They formed a circle around him, their buzzing
whispers adding to the tension of the situation.

"What do you want?" he asked them. His
voice sounded strained, tired.

An older woman, with eyes as green and deep
as the Mediterranean, was the first to step forward, and reached a hand out to the angel warrior. He could see that there were tears in her eyes.

"We want to thank you," she said as she lay a
cool palm against the side of his face, "for saving
our lives."

He looked at her quizzically, her gentle
touch soothing his pain.

"It was one of the fiercest blizzards I can remember," she whispered, tears streaming down her aged face, "and they had come to kill me, their swords of fire sizzling and hissing as the snow fell upon them. As long as I live I'll never forget that sound—or the sound of your voice as you ordered them away from me."

The woman's words gradually sank in. "I . . . I saved you," Camael said, gazing into her bottomless eyes, awash in a sea of emotion.

The woman nodded, a sad smile upon her trembling lips. "Me and so many more," she said, turning to look at the others that crowded behind her.

They all came forward then, hands touching him, the unbridled emotion of their thanks almost intoxicating. How many times had he wondered what became of them; of those half-breeds he had saved from the murderous Powers? How often had he questioned the validity of his mission?

The Nephilim survivors surged around him, the warmth of their gratitude enveloping him in a cocoon of fulfillment.

It wasn't for naught, he thought as he welcomed each word of thanks, every loving touch. Camael, former leader of the Powers host, had at last found his peace, not only in place, but in spirit.

The prisoner curled himself tighter into a ball upon the floor of his cage, his body wracked with painful spasms brought about by the process of healing.

"It's kind of funny," he whispered to the mouse nestled in the crook of his neck, its gentle exhalations soothing in his ear. "Healing hurts almost as much as the injury itself." And again his body twitched and writhed in the throes of repairing itself. He waited for the agony to pass before continuing with his story.

"Sorry about the interruption," he said, trying to focus on something other than the sloughing of his old, dead flesh and the tenderness of the new pink skin beneath. "Where was I?"

The mouse snuffled gently.

"That's right," he answered. "My relationship with the Lord." Another wave of pain swept through his body, and he gritted his teeth and bore the bulk of it before he continued. "I was pretty high on His list of favorites; the mightiest and most beloved of all the angels in Heaven. He called me His Morningstar, and He loved me as much as I loved Him—or so I believed."

And though it was as torturous—even more so than having his burned flesh fall from his body—the prisoner remembered how beautiful it had been. "You should have seen it," he said dreamily, his memories transporting him back to his place of creation, back to Heaven. "It was everything you could possibly dream of—and more. It was Paradise."

He saw again the golden spires of Heaven's celestial mansions, reaching upward into infinity, culminating in the final, seventh Heaven, the place of the highest spiritual perfection. "And that was where He sat, on His throne of light, with me often by His side." The prisoner sighed, pain pulling his thoughts back to reality in his hanging prison.

The mouse was sleeping, but still he heard its voice, its questions about the past and his eventual downfall.

"Do you know I was by His side when He created humanity? The attention He languished on what appeared to us in the heavenly choirs as just another animal!" He remembered his anger, the uncontrollable emotion at the root of his fall so long ago. "He gave them their own paradise, a garden of incredible beauty and bounty. And He gave them something that we did not have. The Creator gave them a piece of Himself, a spark of His divinity—a soul."

The agony of his healing mixed with the recollection of his indignation caused the prisoner to sit bolt upright within the confines of his cage. His hand moved quickly to his bare shoulder, preventing the sleeping rodent from falling. "After all this time it can still get a rise out of me," he said, his voice less raspy, on the mend.

The mouse was in a panic, startled awake by the sudden movement. He could feel the racing beat of its tiny heart against the palm of his hand, the bars of the cage cold against the new flesh of his back.

"I was shocked and horrified, as were others of the various hosts. Why would He give such a priceless gift to a lowly animal? It was an insult to what we were."

The prisoner cupped the fragile creature in the palm of his hand and calmed its jangled nerves with the gentle attentions of his finger.

"Jealousy," he said, a deep sadness permeating the sound of his voice. "Every horrible act that followed was all because of jealousy." In his mind he saw them in the Garden of Eden, man and woman, basking in the light of His glory. "What fragile things they were. And how He loved them—which just made matters all the worse."

The mouse still trembled in his grasp, and the prisoner wondered if it was cold. He held it closer.

"As if things weren't bad enough, it wasn't long before He gathered us together and proclaimed that from that moment forth, we would bow to humanity, we would serve them as we served He who was the Creator of us all."

His scalp began to tingle unpleasantly and he suspected that his hair had begun to grow back.

"Needless to say, several of us were less than thrilled with this new spin on things." He remembered their angry faces again, their indignant fury, but none could match his own. His Lord and Creator had abandoned him, cast him aside for the love of something inferior, and he would not stand for it. "I was so blinded by jealousy and my wounded pride that I gathered an army of those who felt as I did, a third of Heaven's angels they say, and waged war against my heavenly father, my creator, and all those who defended His edict."

Glimpses of a battle fought countless millennia ago danced across his vision of the past. Not a day went by that he didn't relive it. He saw the faces of the elite soldiers, so beautiful and yet so full of rage, and he knew they believed in him, that the cause he fought for was just. "And as the Creator had done with the first humans, I touched them—each and every one of the army that swore their allegiance to me—and I gave them a piece of myself, a fragment of what had once made me the most powerful angel in Heaven." The tips of his fingers came alive with the recollection of those who had received his gift, a black mark—a symbol burned into their flesh, a sigil that spoke of their devotion to him, and to the cause.

"We presumed that the Almighty had no right to do what He did to us—but we presumed too much," the prisoner said sadly. He was exhausted by the painful remembrances of his sordid past; he lowered his hands, and the mouse resting within them, to his lap.

"What were we trying to prove? What were our intentions?" He shook his head and smiled sadly. "Were we going to *force* the Creator to love us best?"

The mouse looked up from the nest within his hands, its dark eyes filled with what he read to be sympathy.

"It was a ferocious battle. I can't even tell you how long it lasted—days, weeks, years perhaps—time passed differently for me then. We fought valiantly, but in the end, it was all in vain."

The mouse nudged at his fingers, its tiny nose a pinprick of cold, and he began to gently pet it again.

"When the battle was finally over, when my elite were dead and myself in chains, I was brought before my Lord God, and finally began to realize the horror of what I had done."

The prisoner closed his eyes to the flood of emotions that filled them, tears streamed down the newly grown skin on his face. "I tried to apologize. I begged for His forgiveness and mercy, but He wouldn't hear it."

A stray tear splashed into his hand and the mouse gingerly licked at the salty fluid.

"I was banished from Heaven, cast down to Earth, and as my constant companion, I would forever experience the pain and suffering of what I had done."

The mouse looked up at him; its triangular head bent quizzically to one side.

"You want to know about the place called Hell?" he asked the curious animal. "There is no Hell," he said. "Hell is in here." He touched the raw, pink skin of his chest with the tips of his fingers. "And it will forever burn inside me for what I have done."

"She said take a left onto Gagnon and there would be a community center where we could get food," Gabriel whined.

"That's what she said," Aaron replied, looking around as they walked. All he could see were homes, each more rundown and dilapidated than the next.

"And what exactly is a community center?" the dog asked pathetically. It was past his suppertime and he was beginning to panic.

Aaron stopped, glancing back in the direction from which they had just come. "This is still Gagnon isn't it?" he asked more to himself then to his ravenous companion.

"I don't know," Gabriel answered, his nose pressed to the sidewalk, searching for the scent of food. *"I'm so hungry I can't even think straight, and it's getting dark."*

They started walking again. A gentle wind blew down the street, rustling what few leaves remained in the skeletal trees.

"Well, let's keep going and see what we run into. Maybe it's at the far end."

"What if it's not?" the dog asked, a touch of

panic in his guttural-sounding voice.

Aaron sighed with exasperation. "Don't worry, Gabe. If we can't find the community center we'll double back to the car, and you can have some of the dog food in the trunk.

"I don't want that food," he said, stopping, ears flat against his blocky head. *"It gives me gas."*

Aaron could not hold back his frustration. "Look, I'm just trying to tell you that you won't starve, okay? You *will* be fed!"

Gabriel's tail began to wag. *"You're a good boy."*

Aaron laughed in spite of himself and motioned for the dog to follow him. "Gabriel, you're a pip!" he said. "C'mon, let's find this place before I starve to death too."

The dog thought for a moment, keeping pace alongside his master. *"I don't think anybody has ever called me a pip before. I've been called a good boy, a good dog, a best pally, but never a pip."*

"Well, there you go," Aaron answered. "Something new for the résumé."

"Do you think we will ever find Stevie?" Gabriel suddenly asked, changing the topic in an instant, as he was prone to do.

Aaron felt his mood suddenly darken. "As soon as we can leave here, we'll start looking again."

"How long will that be?"

Aaron felt himself growing angry again and took a series of deep breaths to calm down. "I don't know," he said flatly. "We'll play by their rules for a while, but there might come a time when we'll have to take a stand."

"I don't like the sound of that," Gabriel said.

"Neither do I," Aaron answered. "Let's just hope it doesn't come to that."

The two continued to walk in brooding silence, both thinking of the disturbing possibilities that waited in their future. They were near the end of the street when Gabriel stopped.

"What is it now?" Aaron snapped.

"Do you smell that?" Gabriel tilted his head back, nose twitching as it pulled something from the air.

Aaron sniffed at the air as well, at first sensing nothing, but then he too smelled it. Food—cooking food.

Gabriel was off in a flash, following the odor as if arrows had been put down on the street to lead them. *"This way,"* he cried excitedly.

Aaron had to quicken his pace to keep up with the hungry animal and watched as Gabriel darted suddenly to the left, moving onto the front lawn of one of the rundown homes.

"This isn't a community center, Gabe," he called, but the dog was in the grip of a food frenzy.

Gabriel followed the scent right up onto the porch and planted his nose at the bottom of the front door, sniffling and snuffling as if it were possible for him to pull some sustenance from beneath the door.

Aaron stood on the walkway. The smell was

stronger and more delicious. He felt his own stomach begin to gurgle. "Gabriel, c'mon down! This is somebody's house."

The Labrador reluctantly turned his head toward Aaron. *"But this house has food."*

Aaron moved closer to the front porch, feeling sorry for the famished animal. "I know there's food here, but we can't just invite ourselves in. Remember, we don't know these people and they probably wouldn't trust us anyway."

"But you're the Chosen One," he said sadly. *"And I'm your dog, who's very hungry."*

If it weren't so pathetic, Aaron probably would have laughed, but the events of the day so far had chased away any chance for humor. "Gabriel, come down here this instant or—"

"Can't we knock and ask where the community center is?" the dog asked with a nervous wag of his muscular tail.

"I guess we could do that," Aaron answered, climbing the three rickety wooden steps to the porch. "But if nobody answers, we have to go. Deal?"

"There's somebody in there, Aaron. I can smell him over the food."

Aaron rapped on the door and waited. He listened for sounds from inside and could just make out the chatter of a television. "I don't think they want to—"

"Knock again," the dog demanded, his tail wagging furiously.

Aaron knocked harder. "Remember what I said: If nobody comes to the door, we go."

Gabriel suddenly bolted down the steps and around the side of the house.

"Where are you going?" Aaron demanded, starting to follow.

"There's somebody in there. Maybe he can hear the back door better," the Lab called excitedly, already out of sight.

Aaron reluctantly followed. He had no idea how the citizens would react if they found him skulking around somebody's home. An image of Lehash with his golden pistols drawn suddenly came to mind. He rounded the corner of the house, careful not to stumble in the growing darkness, and found Gabriel already on the back porch trying to turn the doorknob in his mouth. "What the hell do you think you're doing?"

"I scratched at the door and somebody said come in," Gabriel replied as the door popped open and the rich, succulent smell of cooking food drifted out from the kitchen. Without waiting for an answer, he pushed through the door with his snout and disappeared.

"Gabriel!" Aaron called, climbing the steps and following his dog into the tiny kitchen. It was overly warm and the smell of cooking meat enveloped him like a blanket. Sounds of a television drifted in from the room beyond. "Gabriel, you can't just—"

"I can't help it." Gabriel was moving toward

the stove as if hypnotized, droplets of saliva raining from his mouth to the floor, nose twitching eagerly. *"Maybe he'll invite us to stay."*

"Or he'll call the constables and we'll really be in a fix," Aaron said nervously, half expecting the house's resident to fly into the kitchen screaming.

"I told you he said to come in."

Aaron moved toward the door that would take him out of the kitchen, the light of the television illuminating the room beyond. "Why don't I trust you," he hissed, his back to the animal.

"I don't know." Gabriel sounded hurt.

"Hello?" Aaron called softly as he wrapped his knuckles on the frame of the kitchen doorway. "I don't mean to bother you, but we're looking for the—"

"Come in, Aaron," said a voice from the living room.

Aaron turned back to Gabriel and must have looked surprised.

"I told you he knew we were here," the dog said knowingly.

Aaron walked through a short corridor and into the living room beyond, the sound of Gabriel's toenails clicking on the hardwood floor behind him as he followed. The room was dark except for the flickering light of the television and Aaron could just about make out the older man sitting in a worn, leather recliner in front of an old-fashioned console. It was Belphegor.

Aaron cleared his throat, but the old man did not respond, apparently engrossed in the television show.

Curious, he stepped farther into the room. The sound was turned down, but it looked as though the angel was watching home movies, the scenes jumping from one moment to the next. Suddenly Aaron saw himself on the screen.

He was dressed in a black tuxedo and carrying a flower—a corsage in a clear plastic container. He had just stepped out of his car and was approaching a house that seemed vaguely familiar. *What is this?* His mind was in a panic.

"Aaron, what's wrong?" Gabriel asked, obviously picking up on his panicked vibe.

Aaron could not pull his eyes from the scene unfolding before him. *Where had he seen that house before?* His thoughts raced as he watched himself on the television knocking on the house's front door. It hit him just as the door began to open. It was Belvidere Place back home in Lynn. He'd been there only once before.

The door opened, and Vilma stood there in a cream-colored gown, her hair up and decorated with baby's breath, and the smile on her face as she saw him made him want to cry. His tuxedoed version was in the process of giving her the flower he had brought, when he ripped his eyes from the screen to look at the old man placidly sitting in the oversized chair.

"What is this?" Aaron demanded.

He looked back to the screen briefly to see him and Vilma posing for pictures. Vilma seemed to be embarrassed by the whole thing, waving her family away and trying to drag him toward the car. He couldn't get over how beautiful she looked.

"It's how you wish things had been," Belphegor responded, his eyes never leaving the television. "I like this part . . . didn't take you for a dancer."

Aaron gazed at the set again and saw that he and Vilma were slow dancing among a crowd. He didn't recognize their surroundings, but it appeared to be someplace fancy. Vilma was whispering in his ear as they slowly twirled in a circle on the dance floor. Foolishly he found himself growing jealous of his television doppelgänger. He pulled his eyes away, wanting to look anywhere else but there. His eyes landed on the dark cord of the television lying upon the floor, curled like a resting snake.

"It's not plugged in," he said aloud, turning his full attention to Belphegor. "The television's not plugged in."

"This is what your life could have been if not for the power that awakened inside you."

He didn't want to, but Aaron found himself looking at the screen again. He saw himself in a cap and gown, a stupid-looking grin on his face, accepting his diploma from Mr. Costan.

The view suddenly turned to the auditorium

audience. With a sickening feeling growing in the pit of his stomach, he watched his foster mom and dad proudly applaud his achievement. It was when he noticed Stevie sitting in the chair beside his mother, smiling as if he didn't have a problem in the world, that he realized he'd had more than enough.

"Make it stop," he demanded, stepping farther into the room, fists clenched. He felt the manacles around his wrists and the collar about his neck grow warmer.

Belphegor didn't respond, smiling as he watched television. Aaron couldn't help himself and chanced a quick glance. It was like driving past a car accident. You didn't want to see—but you just had to look. He appeared older now, sitting in a large classroom taking notes as a professor lectured. He was in college, and a part of him longed to switch places with this version of himself.

"I've seen enough," he said louder, more demanding. The restraints were burning him, but he barely noticed, for his angelic nature had been awakened by his anger and it coiled within him, eager to strike.

"Isn't this what you wanted, Aaron?" Belphegor asked, pointing to the TV.

Aaron didn't want to see, but it was as if he weren't in control of his movements. He was giving Vilma a ring. They were on a beach at sunset. Gabriel, looking older but still active, was happily chasing seagulls, and Vilma was sitting on a blanket with him. There was love in her eyes—love for him—and even though the sound was off, he knew his words at that moment. *Will you marry me?*

The angelic nature within him screamed, hurling itself against the restraints of the magicks within the golden metal that bound him. The pain was incredible, and he began to scream, but more from anger than hurt.

Gabriel began to panic and fled into the kitchen, barking as he ran.

"Turn it off! Turn it off! Turn it off!" Aaron demanded, his voice raw and filled with emotion. "I don't want to see this—I don't want to see what I can't ever have. Why are you doing this?"

He stumbled forward to block the set, catching sight of Vilma in a wedding gown as she walked down the aisle of a church. His skin was on fire, the alien symbols appearing upon his flesh, even though the magick within the restraints tried to stop it. The wings beneath the flesh of his back writhed in agitation, gradually moving to the surface, ready to unfurl.

"I have to see if it's true," Belphegor said calmly. "I have to see if you are indeed the One."

Something inside Aaron broke. There was a sound in his head like the scream of high-speed train, and his wings exploded from his back, as the power of an angel suddenly flowed unimpeded from his body. As if suddenly made ancient and brittle, the manacles upon his wrists and the collar about his neck broke, crumbling as dust to the floor. A sword of fire ignited in his hand and, gazing greedily upon its destructive potential, he spun around, bringing the burning blade down upon the wooden cabinet of the television console. The window into a life he would never know exploded in flames and a shower of glass, but not before he glimpsed a very pregnant Vilma, smiling as if she somehow knew he was watching.

The transformed Aaron, his wings of glistening black spread wide, turned back to glare at Belphegor, who still sat quietly in his recliner. Gabriel tentatively peered around the doorway from the kitchen, ears flat against his square head.

"Are . . . are you all right, Aaron?" the dog asked.

"I'm fine, Gabriel," Aaron growled in the voice of the Nephilim. He pointed his sword of orange flame at the fallen angel. "You wanted to know if I was the One," he said, voice booming about the confines of the room. "Well, what do you think?"

"I think that supper's just about ready," Belphegor responded with a soothing smile, rising from his chair. "Would you and your friend care to join me?"

Gabriel pushed the plate of mashed potatoes, gravy, and peas farther across the dining room floor with each consecutive lap of his muscular tongue. Before he wound up halfway across the house, Aaron reached down and took the plate away.

"*I'm not finished with that,*" the dog said, the remains of mashed potatoes decorating the top of his nose.

"Believe me, you're finished," Aaron said, setting the spotless plate on the tabletop. *The plate is so clean, Belphegor could put it away without washing it,* he thought. *No one would be the wiser.*

"*I would like some more,*" Gabriel said with a wag of his tail.

"You've had enough," Aaron responded, as he took a hearty bite of his own roast beef and gravy. Then, always the ultimate pushover, he picked up a piece of meat from his plate and fed it to his insatiable companion. "Watch the fingers!" he squealed as the animal snatched away his offering. "I still use those, thank you very much."

Belphegor walked in from the kitchen with another steaming bowl in his hands. "Here are some fresh green beans," he said as he placed it on the table. "I grew them myself."

"Here?" Aaron asked, shaking his head. "No, thank you. I'm not into toxic waste."

"*I like toxic waste,*" Gabriel said happily, attempting to lick the remains of potato from his nose.

"It's perfectly safe," Belphegor said as he pulled out a chair and sat down across from

Aaron. "All the poisons have been removed. They're quite good."

Aaron was reaching for the beans when he realized that Belphegor did not have a plate. "Aren't you eating?"

The angel shook his head. "No, not tonight. I actually prefer preparing meals to eating them." The fallen angel smiled, watching as Aaron spooned a heaping portion of the rich green vegetable onto his plate.

"You are aware that we—of my kind—do not need to eat."

"I've heard," Aaron said taking a careful bite of the beans and then eagerly having more. "Except that Camael has a thing for French fries now."

Belphegor sat back in his chair. "Does he? I would never have imagined that. Perhaps the years upon this world have indeed softened our Powers' commander."

"*Former* commander," Aaron corrected through a mouthful of food. "Verchiel's the commander now—and has been for quite some time."

"Of course," Belphegor answered, crossing his arms. "How foolish of me to forget."

His plate nearly as clean as Gabriel's bowl, Aaron had a drink of water from an old jelly jar, then pushed the utensils away. "That thing with the television," he asked. "How did you do that?"

Gabriel had finally settled down and lay

beside Aaron's chair. Aaron reached down to pet his friend as he waited for an answer.

"You wouldn't believe it if I told you." Belphegor shook his head, arms still crossed.

"You'd be surprised at the things I believe in now," Aaron said. Gabriel rolled onto his side to expose his belly, and Aaron obliged the animal. "Were those . . . images, those scenes . . . were they from some future or—"

"They were taken from your head and manipulated," Belphegor answered, tapping a finger against his skull. "Things that you most desire, but will likely never achieve."

Aaron stopped scratching Gabriel's belly, earning a disappointed snuff, and leaned back in his chair. "I don't like to think that way," he said, eyes focused on his empty plate, but seeing something else—a future that could very well be like the one he'd seen on Belphegor's television. "I like to think that there's something more for me, after I find my brother and this whole prophecy thing gets straightened out."

Belphegor chuckled. "Don't worry yourself about the prophecy thing," he said as he stood up from his chair. He started to gather the dirty bowls and plates.

"Why's that?"

The old fallen angel used a spoon to scrape what remained of the mashed potatoes onto Aaron's dirty plate. "Because it doesn't concern you," he answered.

"Don't you think I'm the One?" Aaron asked curiously, leaning forward in his seat. "You heard what Camael said, and you saw what I did to your magick handcuffs."

"All very impressive." Belphegor nodded as he gave Gabriel a green bean from the plate of refuse. "I can honestly say that I've never seen power the likes of yours, and your control over it thus far is admirable, but I do not believe you are the One spoken of in prophecy."

Aaron was surprised by the disappointment he felt; a day ago he would have traded the whole angelic Chosen One thing for a bag of Doritos. *Now . . .* "Are you positive?" he asked. "How do you know? Camael said . . ."

"Camael has been separated from his kind for a very long time," the angel explained, pausing in his cleanup to gaze intently at Aaron. "He is desperate to belong again—perhaps too desperate—and he saw something in you that really isn't there. I'm sorry."

There was something in Belphegor's attitude that suddenly annoyed Aaron. It reminded him of his childhood in foster care, before he moved to the Stanleys' and learned what being part of a family was all about. Before that he was looked on as being less than other kids, perceived as a failure before he even had a chance to try.

"The essence inside you is extremely powerful, and I fear that if a true merger were ever to occur between the angelic nature and your fragile human psyche, you would be driven out of your mind. And we of Aerie would be forced to do something about it."

Aaron remembered a teacher he'd had in the first grade, Mr. Laidon. The teacher had singled him out, telling the other students that he didn't have a family and that the state needed to take care of him. At that moment he had felt like a show-and-tell project, something less than the other kids in his class. Aaron's face flushed hot with the memory.

"Maybe I could be taught," he began. "Camael says that if a union occurs properly—"

The old angel chuckled, a condescending laugh that Aaron had heard so many times in his life.

"Teach you to be our messiah?" Belphegor asked. "No, Aaron. The true One spoken of in our sacred writing will be coming, just not right now."

"But the Archangel Gabriel said that I was God's new messenger," Aaron argued.

"Then he was wrong," Belphegor emphatically stated, and picked up the dishes, signaling an end to the conversation.

Aaron felt empty, as if being the savior of the fallen had actually begun to mean something to him, warts and all. He was about to offer Belphegor some help when there came a frantic rapping at the front door. Gabriel immediately sprang to his feet and began to bark.

"Come in," Belphegor called out, turning toward the front door, arms loaded with dirty dishes.

They heard the sounds of the front door open and close, followed by rapid footsteps. Scholar rushed in through the living room clutching a notebook in one hand. "Belphegor we need to speak at once. . . ." His eyes found Aaron's and he fell silent.

"Good evening, Scholar. Aaron and I were just having dinner. May I get you something? Some coffee, or maybe some pie?"

The silence was becoming uncomfortable when Scholar finally spoke. "I need to speak with you in private, Belphegor." He tore his eyes from Aaron's and raised the notebook toward the old angel.

"Come with me," Belphegor said. "Excuse us for a moment, Aaron."

The two left the dining room, leaving Aaron to wonder what had gotten the angel so riled.

"So you're not the Chosen One, then?" Gabriel said, distracting him from his thoughts.

"I thought you were asleep," Aaron said, leaning back in his chair and watching the doorway to the kitchen.

"You'd be surprised what I hear when I'm asleep."

"He doesn't think that it's me. It's no big deal. I always knew there was a chance that Camael was full of it." He looked at his dog lying on the floor by his chair.

"What does this mean for us now?" Gabriel asked earnestly.

Aaron shrugged. "I don't really know," he said, for the first time in a long while considering a future that didn't involve the angelic prophecy. "I guess it means we can get out of here and get back to finding Stevie."

"Do you think Camael will come with us?"

Aaron didn't get a chance to answer, for at that moment Belphegor and Scholar returned to the room. There was a strange look upon the old angel's face and Aaron saw that he was holding Scholar's notebook. It was open and Aaron could see parts of drawings that he recognized, sketches of the symbols that appeared on his body when he allowed his angelic essence to emerge.

"Is everything all right?" Aaron asked. As of late, fearing the worst had become as natural to him as breathing. It wasn't the greatest way to be, but at least he was always prepared.

"Were you serious about being taught, about wanting to learn?" Belphegor questioned.

Aaron nodded, not quite sure what he was getting himself into.

Belphegor handed the notebook and its drawings back to Scholar. "We'll begin your training immediately."

chapter seven

Camael sat on the forest green, metal bench in the tiny playground, his angel eyes detecting the resonance of things long past—ghosts of children and families who had once played here. It had been seven days since he and Aaron first arrived in Aerie, and the former leader of the Powers was having to deal with ghosts of his own. He thought of those he had destroyed during the conflict in Heaven, and those slain after the war when he was performing his duty as commander of the Powers host—obliterating those who were an offense to the Creator. Since finding Aerie, he'd been thinking of them more and more, their faces and death cries haunting his every moment.

Should I be allowed to stay here? he wondered. For if he had found this place before his change of heart, before the realization that the killing had to stop, he would have razed it, burned it to ash in a rain of heavenly fire—and God have mercy upon those he found living within its confines.

A crow cried overhead as it circled a gnarled and diseased tree growing to the side of the play area. Its caws voiced its uneasiness with the area, despite the fact that it was tired and wanted to rest. The animals knew that the Ravenschild development was poisoned, Camael realized; they could taste its taint on the air rising up from the earth. The place had the stink of man's folly, and the blackbird, knowing it did not belong here, flew on in search of another place to rest its tired wings.

Do I belong? Camael deliberated. He had searched for Aerie for many hundreds of years, but had he actually earned a place here? The faces of those who fell before him were slowly pushed aside, replaced by those he had saved. He could still hear their plaintive words of thanks and feel their touches of gratitude. Despite the violence he had wrought in the ancient past, he had still managed to do some good, and he would need to hold on to that as a drowning man would latch on to debris adrift in storm-wracked seas.

And what about the Creator? His mind frothed with questions for which he did not have answers. *Does He look upon me with disdain, or pity? When the time comes, will I be permitted to go home?*

The sound of claws upon the tar path interrupted the angel's musings, and he turned to see Gabriel trotting toward him.

"Camael, have you seen Aaron?" the dog asked, stopping before the bench.

The angel shook his head. "Not since this morning. I believe he is still with Belphegor."

"It figures," Gabriel responded morosely.

"Is there a problem?" Camael asked, curious in spite of himself.

The dog hopped up onto the bench and sat beside him. *"He's never around anymore. I see him early in the morning when he takes me out and gets my breakfast, but then he's gone all day and he's too tired to play when he gets back."*

Camael slid over on the bench, away from the dog. He and Gabriel had developed a grudging respect for each other, but he still did not like to be too close to the animal. "I believe that Belphegor is attempting to train Aaron in the use of his angelic abilities."

"And that's something else I don't understand," said the dog indignantly. *"First they think Aaron is a lost cause and now they can't seem to get enough of him. Besides, I thought you were training Aaron."*

"It would seem that Belphegor and the others have at last seen in Aaron what I found several weeks ago," Camael explained. "What that something is I cannot tell you, but it was enough to gain their trust and free us from those damnable restraints." The angel unconsciously rubbed at his wrists where the magickal manacles had recently been removed.

They were silent for a moment, two unlikely comrades pondering a similar mystery.

"I miss him, Camael," Gabriel said as he gazed into the playground. *"I feel as if I'm losing him."*

"If Aaron is indeed the One foretold of in prophecy, you are losing him to something far larger than your simple emotional needs. He will be the one that brings about our redemption—Heaven will open its arms to us again and welcome us home," Camael said.

Gabriel turned his head to look at the angel. His animal eyes seemed darker somehow, intense with worry. *"I don't care about redemption,"* the Labrador said with a tremble in his voice. *"He was mine first; Aaron belongs to me."*

The primitive bond between humans and their domesticated animals was something that Camael had always struggled to understand. How had Aaron defined it for him during one of their seemingly endless drives? Unconditional love, he believed was how the boy had phrased it. The master was the animal's whole world, and it would love its master no matter what. That was the strength of the bond. The angel found the level of loyalty quite amazing.

"Aaron does not belong to you alone, Gabriel," Camael explained. "There are those around us now who have waited for his arrival for thousands of years. Would you deny them his touch?"

The dog bowed his head, golden brown ears pressed flat against his skull. *"No,"* Gabriel growled, *"but who will take care of me if something happens to him?"*

Camael had no idea how to respond. It was a variation of a question he had been wondering himself. If Aaron was indeed the Chosen, what fate would the fallen meet if Verchiel should succeed in his mad plans to see the Nephilim destroyed?

The two sat quietly on the bench, the weight of their questions heavy upon their thoughts, the answers as elusive as the future.

Lorelei stepped out the back door of the house she shared with Lehash, a steaming cup of coffee in one hand, searching for her father. She thought the constable had come outside, but he was nowhere to be seen. Since the strangers' arrival, Lehash had become distant, uncommunicative, immersed in his work of keeping the citizens of Aerie safe, and she was becoming concerned.

Over the sound of the gas-powered generator that provided their electricity, she heard the reports of his guns, like small claps of thunder, rolling up from somewhere beyond the thick brush that surrounded the backyard. She started toward the sound, dipping her head beneath young saplings, careful not to spill the coffee as she maneuvered through the woods. Stepping into a man-made clearing, probably meant for development in years past, Lorelei stared at her father's back as he fired at targets set up along the far side of the wide open space. The weapons discharged with a booming report, and several targets disintegrated in plumes of heavenly fire.

"Good shootin', Tex," she joked, letting him know that he was no longer alone.

Lehash slowly turned and regarded her with dark and somber eyes, smoking pistols of gold in each hand. It was a look common to the head constable of Aerie, a look that she herself was often accused of wearing. The angel Lehash took everything quite seriously.

"Practicing?" she asked, moving closer and holding out the steaming mug of coffee.

He pointed a pistol over his shoulder and fired. Lorelei jumped as an old teddy bear tied to a tree exploded in a cloud of burning stuffing.

"Well, it does make perfect," he said, the slightest hint of a Texas twang in his voice. It never ceased to amuse her how he insisted on hanging on to the mannerisms and style of the old West. He'd explained that it had been his favorite time period during his countless years on Earth, and she guessed it was better than if he'd fallen in love with the Bronze age.

The golden pistols shimmered and disappeared into the ether with a flash of flame, and Lehash took the mug from her.

"And here I thought you were already perfect," she said, placing her hands inside the front pockets of her jeans. "Guess you really do learn something new every day."

He sipped at the coffee carefully, ignoring her good-natured barb. Something was bothering him, and now was as good a time as any to find out what.

"What's the matter, Lehash?" she asked. "Something's got your dander up even more than usual."

The angel looked up into the early morning, powder blue sky, as if searching for something. "Belphegor's been talking 'bout how he thinks trouble's coming." He took another swig of coffee and glanced back to her. "I believe it's already here."

She was confused at first, but then realized the meaning of his words. "You can't blame Aaron and Camael anymore. The deaths of other fallen have continued around the world since they've been here. And besides, reports that have trickled in say that the killer wears armor— blood-red armor." Lorelei felt a chill creep down her spine and shivered.

"And our troubles are just beginning," Lehash said, finishing the last of his drink. "Kind of like the early tremors I felt that morning in San Francisco in 1906—and we know how that one turned out."

Lorelei sighed, her father often used historical catastrophes to make his points; the *Hindenburg* and *Titanic* disasters were quite popular with him, as were the Boxer Rebellion and World War II.

"Did you ever stop to think that their coming might be the beginning of something good?" she asked. "Y'know there's talk among the citizens that . . ." Lorelei stopped, suddenly not sure if she should continue.

"Talk about what?" he asked, his voice a low rumble, its tone already telling her that he wasn't going to care for what she had to say.

"That Aaron . . . that he might really be the One."

Lehash scowled and handed her back the empty mug. The golden pistols formed in his hands again, and he turned away to resume his target practice.

"What's the matter?" she asked. "What could possibly be wrong if that were true?"

Lehash did not answer her in words. Instead he began to fire his weapons repeatedly, with barely a moment between each of the thunderous blasts. The remaining targets disintegrated, as did the trees and branches that they had been positioned upon.

Then, as quickly as he had begun to fire, he stopped, whirling around to face her. "You haven't seen what I've seen, Lore. I've been living for a very long time now, and the thought of some messiah suddenly making everything all better . . ." He shook his head.

Lorelei moved toward him, words of disbelief

spilling from her lips. "Are you saying you don't believe in the prophecy?" she asked incredulously. "The whole reason that Aerie even exists, and you don't believe in it?"

He lowered the smoldering weapons, and held her in his steely gaze. "Aerie and its people are about the only things I *do* believe in these days."

Lorelei was speechless. She had only learned of the prophecy on her arrival in Ravenschild, but the promise of something other than the harsh world that she'd grown up in had given her the strength to continue.

"I fought during the Great War, Lorelei," he tried to explain. "And not on the winning side. I can't believe that God—even one merciful and just—could ever begin to forgive us for the wrong we've done."

She didn't want to hear this; she didn't want the hope that she kept protected deep inside her to be diminished in any way.

"The prophecy says—"

"Fairy stories," he retorted. The guns had again disappeared, and he grasped her shoulders in a powerful grip. "What you've got to realize—what we've all got to realize—is the only thing we have to look forward to is a world of hurt, and not all the prophecies and teenage messiahs in the world are gonna keep it away."

"But what if you're wrong?" she asked, pulling away. "What if Aaron *is* the harbinger of better times?"

Lehash scowled. "If you believe that, then I have some serious doubts as to whether you really are my daughter."

The words of a powerful angelic spell that would have caused the ground to split beneath the fallen angel and swallow him whole, danced at the edge of her mind. It was ready to spill from her lips, but Lorelei stopped herself, instead turning her back upon her parent and starting back to the house. As she made her way through the brush, a part of her wished for him to call after her, to apologize in a fatherly way for the harshness of his words, but the more realistic half got exactly what it expected.

He had begun his target practice again, the blasts of gunfire like the explosive precursor to an approaching storm.

Vilma Santiago felt her eyes grow increasingly heavy, the words of text in her literature book starting to blur. She refused to look at the clock, deluding herself into thinking that if she didn't know the time, her body wouldn't crave sleep as badly. She thought about taking another of the pills she had bought at the drugstore to keep herself awake, but she'd already had three, and the directions said no more than two were recommended.

She closed her literature book and slid it into the bag leaning against the side of her desk. *Maybe if I can get ahead on my physics assignments,*

Vilma thought, pulling out the overly large book and placing it on the desk before her.

Vilma would do anything to stay awake, anything to avoid the dreams. Disturbing visions from her recurring nightmares flashed before her eyes, a staccato slideshow of images that seemed more like memories than the fantastic creations of a sleeping mind. She felt herself begin to slip into the fugue state that always preceded sleep, and spastically jumped from her chair. Pacing about her bedroom, she slapped at her cheeks, hoping that the sharp stabs of pain would give her a second wind. *Or would this be my third?* she wondered groggily.

"C'mon, Vilma," she said aloud. "Stay awake." From the corner of her eye she saw her bed and for a split second could have sworn that it was calling to her. "No," she said. "No bed, you know what it means when you go to bed." She continued to pace, swinging her arms and taking deep breaths.

As she walked around her room, Vilma saw that a pink envelope had fallen from her book bag when she'd removed her physics text. It was a birthday card from Tina, who wasn't going to be in school the next day and hadn't wanted to miss her friend's big day. Vilma was going to be eighteen years old, but if it hadn't been for Tina, she wouldn't have even remembered. She retrieved the envelope and opened it. It was a typical Tina card. "I know what would make your birthday happy!" read the caption over a picture of a man wearing only unzipped blue jeans, his abs and pecs spectacularly oiled.

"You think so?" Vilma asked the card as she studied the handsome figure. She immediately thought of Aaron. It had been two weeks since his last e-mail and she was beginning to fear that she'd never hear from him again, that maybe he had found a new life somewhere, and no longer wanted reminders of the past he had left behind.

Vilma pushed the horrible thought from her head as she tossed the card into the plastic barrel beside her desk. *He probably just hasn't had a chance to get to a computer.* In fact she wouldn't be surprised if there was a message from him now. She had checked her e-mail just a few hours ago, but something told her that *maybe* Aaron had been in touch since then.

Vilma returned to her desk and turned on the computer. As she waited for the system to boot up, her thoughts stayed on the boy who had captured her heart. She wondered how he would react if she told him about her awful dreams and her fear of sleep—and would she even share the information with him in the first place? The answer to that was a simple one: of course she would. The way she felt about Aaron Corbet, she would have told him anything. It was as if they shared some strange kind of bond.

Maneuvering her mouse she clicked on the icon to connect to the Internet. *Maybe he sent me an electronic greeting card*, she thought happily and then realized that he probably didn't even know that tomorrow was her birthday. From the living room downstairs, the old grandfather clock began to chime, and as she waited for her connection, Vilma found herself counting the tolls of the bell.

Bong! Bong! Bong! Bong! Bong! Bong! Bong! Bong! Bong! Bong! Bong!

The clock tolled midnight, and she saw that there were no messages from Aaron or anybody else. Vilma was overcome with disappointment and the realization that she was now a year older. She stared at the computer screen, wishing a message to appear, but it didn't happen. "Happy Birthday to me," she said sadly.

She prepared to disconnect from the Internet and her bleary eyes traveled to the right corner of the screen where it showed the time. The clock read 11:59 P.M. and she offhandedly wondered if the clock downstairs was fast, or her computer's clock slow. Then, just as the disconnect message came up, the clock on her screen changed to 12:00 A.M.—and every one of her senses inexplicably came alive at once.

Vilma tossed her head violently back and the chair tipped over, spilling her onto the floor. The assault came upon her in waves. The sounds in her ears were deafening, a cacophony of noise through which she could just hear the panicked beat of her own heart and the swishing of blood through her veins.

What's happening to me? Vilma thought as she struggled to her feet, her hands pressed tightly against the bludgeoning invasion of sound. *Is this some kind of bizarre reaction to my lack of sleep, or the drugs I've taken?* she frantically wondered. Smells were suddenly overpowering—cleaning products from the kitchen, wood stain from the basement, bags of garbage in the barrels outside. She gasped for breath. The light of the room was blinding, and she lashed out at the lamp on her desk, knocking it to the floor.

I've got to get help! Vilma panicked. She needed a hospital. . . . She would wake her aunt and uncle. . . .

Her hand was on the doorknob when she heard a voice from somewhere in the room behind her. *"The seed of a seraph stirs to waking as the clock tolls twelve,"* it said in a language that she had never heard before and should not have been able to understand—but did. *"This new day is the day of your birth, I'd wager."*

The hairs at the back of Vilma's neck bristled. She didn't want to turn around, didn't want to acknowledge this latest bit of insanity, but she could not help herself. As she slowly began to turn, a strange odor suddenly permeated the air. It smelled of rich spice and something rotten. It smelled of decay.

Vilma saw that there was a man inside her bedroom. He was dressed in dark clothes and wore a long raincoat despite the fact that it had not rained in weeks. His hair was long and combed back upon his head. His skin was deathly pale and seemed to glow in the limited light, and his eyes, if he had any, were lost within dark shadows that sat upon his face. Vilma had seen this mysterious figment of her madness before, perched in the tree outside her window: watching, waiting.

"You're not real."

"Think what you will," he answered in the ancient tongue as he started toward her. *"It is no concern of mine. My charge was to wait and watch for you to blossom—and that is exactly what you have started to do."*

She closed her eyes and wished the figure away, but still he moved toward her. A scream about to explode from her lips froze in her lungs, and Vilma watched in stunned silence as speckled wings of black and white gradually unfurled from the figure's back.

"Come along, little Nephilim," said the man who could only have been an angel. *"My master has plans for you."*

He took her in his arms and the world around her began to spin. And as she fell into unconsciousness, Vilma Santiago wondered if she was being taken to meet with God.

chapter eight

Belphegor walked among his crops and in the primitive language of the bug, kindly asked them to leave his vegetables. Purging his gardens of toxic residue was like placing neon signs in front of all his plants, welcoming the various insects. But he hadn't forgotten them. There was an area of garden he had grown especially for the primitive life forms, and he invited them to partake of that particular bounty. The insects did as he asked, some flying into the air in a buzzing cloud, while others tumbled to the rich earth, heading for a more appropriate place to dine. The bugs did not care where they ate, as long as they were allowed to feed.

The angel thanked the simple creatures and turned his attention to a pitcher of iced tea that was waiting for him atop a rusted patio table in the center of the yard. He strolled casually through the grass, his bare feet enjoying the sensation of the new, healthy plant life. Removing the poisons from the backyards of Ravenschild brought him great pleasure, although those same toxins were beginning to wear upon his own body. The angel poured himself a glass from the pitcher of brown liquid and gazed out over his own little piece of paradise as he drank. This yard, of all the yards in Aerie, was one of his favorites. He had made it his own and it was good again. If only it was as simple for those who had fallen from God's grace.

And then came that odd feeling of excitement he'd experienced since first viewing the manifestation of Aaron Corbet's angelic self. *Is it possible?* Could he dare to believe that after all this time, after so many false hopes, the prophecy might actually come true?

Belphegor sipped his bitter brew, enjoying the sensation of the cold fluid as it traveled down his throat. He would not allow himself to be tricked; there was too much—too many—relying upon him, to be caught up in a wave of religious fervor. But he had to admit, there was something about this Nephilim, something wild, untamed, that inspired both excitement and fear.

The teaching had been going reasonably well. The boy was eager to learn, but his angelic nature was rough, rebellious, and if they were not careful, a deadly force could be unleashed upon them—upon the world. But that was a worry for another time.

The air in a far corner of the yard began to shimmer, a dark patch forming at the center of the distress. There was sound, very much like the inhalation of breath, and the darkness blossomed to reveal its identity. Wings that seemed to be made from swaths of solid night unfurled, the shape of the boy nestled between them. He looked exhausted, yet exhilarated, a cocky smile on his young face.

"That took longer than I expected," Belphegor said, feigning disinterest as he reached for the pitcher of iced tea and refilled his glass. "Was there a problem?"

Aaron suppressed his angelic nature, the sigils fading, the wings shrinking to nothing upon his back. In his hand he held a rolled newspaper and whacked it against the palm of his other hand as he walked toward the old angel. "No problems," he said, tossing the paper onto the patio table where it unrolled to reveal the Chinese typesetting. It was *The People's Daily*. "I didn't have any Chinese money to buy one, so I had to wait until somebody threw this away."

The boy smiled, exuding a newfound confidence. He was learning fast, but there was still much to do—and so many ways in which things could go wrong.

"How was the travel?" Belphegor asked before taking another sip of tea. He had taught the youth a method of angelic travel requiring only the wings on his back and an idea of where he wanted to go.

"It was amazing," Aaron said. There was another glass on the table and he reached for it. "I did exactly what you said." He poured a full glass, almost spilling it in his excitement. "I pictured Beijing in my head, from those travel books and magazines, and I told myself that was where I wanted to be."

Belphegor nodded, secretly impressed. There had been many a Nephilim that couldn't even begin to grasp the concept, never mind actually do it.

"It was pretty cool," Aaron continued. "I saw it in my head, wrapped myself in my wings, and when I opened them up again, I was there." He gulped down his iced tea.

"And did anyone notice your arrival?"

Aaron tapped the remainder of the ice cubes in his glass into his open mouth and began to crunch noisily. "Nope," he said between crunches. "I didn't want anybody to see me—so they didn't."

Belphegor turned away and strolled back toward his plants and vegetables, leaving Aaron alone by the table. Absently he began to harvest some ripened cucumbers. The boy was advancing far more quickly than any Nephilim he had ever encountered. But the next phase of training was crucial, and the most dangerous. Despite his affinity, Belphegor wasn't sure if Aaron was ready.

"So what now?" he heard Aaron ask behind him.

Belphegor stopped and turned, cucumbers momentarily forgotten. "We're done for the day," he said dismissively.

"But it's still early," the Nephilim said, genuine eagerness in his voice. "Isn't there something more you can show me before—"

"The next phase of development is the investigation of your inner self," the angel interrupted.

"Okay," Aaron responded easily. "Let's do it."

"Do you think you're ready for a trip inside here?" Belphegor tapped Aaron's chest. "It's going to be a lot harder than a jaunt to Beijing."

Aaron's expression became more serious, as if the angel's cautioning words had stirred something—some shaded information hidden in the back of Aaron's mind, about to be dragged out into the light.

"If you think you're ready, prepared to find out who you are . . . what you are," Belphegor said cryptically, holding the boy in an unwavering gaze, "then, we'll begin. But I'm not entirely sure you'll be happy with what you learn."

Verchiel gazed upon the unconscious female who had been laid on the floor before him. "Can you sense it as I can?" he asked the prisoner in the hanging cage across the room. "Like a newly emerging hatchling, fighting against the shell of its humanity. It wants so desperately to be free of its confines, to blossom and transform its fragile human vessel into the horror it is destined to be."

The leader of the Powers shifted his weight uncomfortably in the high-backed wooden chair. Though finally healing, the burns that he had received in his first confrontation with the Nephilim still caused him a great deal of discomfort. "It sickens me," Verchiel spat, his eyes riveted to the girl at his feet. "I should kill the wretched thing now."

"But you won't," wheezed the prisoner, still weak. "You took the trouble to bring her here, I gather she's going to play a part in whatever new trick you have up your sleeve. Maybe bait, to lure the Nephilim into a trap?"

Verchiel turned his attention from the girl to the prisoner. "Are you learning to think like me?" he asked with a humorless smile. "Or am I starting to think like you?"

The prisoner raised himself to a sitting position. "I'm not sure that even in my darkest days I could muster such disregard for innocent life."

"Innocent life?" the leader of the Powers asked as he studied the creature before him. "So simple—so defenseless—one can almost see why the Creator was so taken with them."

The female moaned softly in the grip of oblivion.

"But looks can be deceiving, can they not?" He nudged the girl with his foot. "There is a monster inside you just waiting to come out, isn't there, girl?"

The captive gripped the bars of his cage, hands pink with a fresh layer of skin. "A little bit of the pot calling the kettle black, don't you think, Verchiel?" he asked. "After all you've done of late, do you really believe she deserves the title of monster?"

Verchiel tilted his head in thought as he studied the girl lying before him. "I am not without a certain measure of pity for the misfortune of her birth. She cannot help what she is, but it does not change the fact that the likes of her kind should not exist."

"And who exactly provided you with this information?" the captive asked. "'Cause it looks as though I might have missed the announcement."

"It was never intended for our kind to lay with animals," Verchiel growled, the concept flooding him with feelings of revulsion. "The proof is in these monstrosities—animals with the power of the divine. I cannot imagine it was ever a part of the Creator's plan."

"And you being so close to God and all, you've taken it upon yourself to clear up the problem."

"As impudent as ever," Verchiel said, sliding from the chair to kneel beside the unconscious girl. "One would think that after all this time you would have learned some modicum of respect for the One you so horribly wronged."

"This has nothing to do with Him, Verchiel," the prisoner stressed, "and everything to do with your twisted perception of right and wrong."

Verchiel stifled the urge to lash out at his captive, focusing instead on the task at hand. "Right and wrong," he hissed, as he pushed up the girl's shirt to reveal the dark, delicate skin of her young stomach. "What is coming to fruition inside this poor creature is wrong."

The fingers of Verchiel's hand began to glow, and he lightly touched her stomach, burning her flesh in five places. Even within the hold of unconsciousness the female cried out, writhing in agony as her flesh sizzled and wisps of oily smoke curled up from the burns.

"I know what I do is right," he said. "There is a bond between the Nephilim and this female, a bond that will only be made stronger with the realization that they are of the same kind."

Verchiel could sense the essence of angel coiled inside the young woman, still not fully awake. The pain would draw it closer, forcing it to blossom sooner. He again reached down and touched her stomach, leaving his fingertips upon the fragile flesh just a bit longer. The fluids within the skin sputtered, crackled, and popped with his hellish caress.

The girl was moaning and crying now, still

not fully awake, but the power inside her was growing stronger, calling out to others of its ilk for help.

"That's it," Verchiel cooed, inhaling the acrid aroma of burning skin. "Summon the great hero to your side so that I may destroy him and the dreams he inspires."

It was like the dreams. . . . No, *nightmares*, he had been having before the change.

But Aaron was not asleep.

Belphegor had done this. He had taken Aaron into his home, telling him he had to learn the origins of the angelic essence that had become a part of him. He had made him drink a mug of some awful-tasting concoction from a boiling pot on the stove. It tasted like garbage and smelled even worse, but the old fallen angel had said that it would help Aaron to travel inside himself, to experience the genesis of the power that wanted so desperately to reshape him.

Aaron had choked down the foul liquid and sat upon the living-room floor, while Belphegor took his place in the recliner and began to read *The People's Daily*. At first Aaron was concerned that nothing was happening, but the old fallen angel had looked over the top of the paper and told him to wait for the poison to take effect.

Poison?

Yes, Belphegor had indeed given him poison—the impending death of his human aspect would allow his angelic nature to assume control, Belphegor explained before going back to the news of China.

A stabbing pain had begun in the pit of his stomach. An unnatural warmth radiated from the center of the intense agony and spread through his extremities, numbing them. Aaron found that he could no longer sit up and fell to his side on the cold wooden floor.

He was finding it hard to stay conscious, but could still hear Belphegor encouraging him to hold on, warning him not to succumb fully to the poison coursing through his body. Aaron had to find the source of his essence's power; then wrest control away from the strengthening angelic might, and use it to complete the unification of the dual natures that existed within him.

What if I'm not strong enough? Aaron had asked. And the old angel had looked at him grimly and said that without the anchor of his humanity, the angelic essence within him would surely run amok and destroy them all.

At first there was only darkness and the burning warmth of the poison, but then he saw it there, writhing in the black sea of his gradual demise. When Aaron had last seen it, the power had taken the shapes of various creatures of creation. Now it had matured into a beautiful winged creature, humanoid in shape, with skin the color of the sun and eyes as cool and dark as the night. They were family in a strange kind of way, he thought, and it drew him close, wrapping him in its embrace, flowing over and into him as if liquid, and when he opened his eyes, he was somewhere else entirely.

The pain of the poison was gone and Aaron found himself standing in a vast field of tall grass the color of gold. A warm gentle breeze smelling of rich spice caressed the waving plains. Far off in the distance he could just about make out the shape of a vast city, but there were sounds nearby that pulled his attention away from the metropolis. He turned and walked toward a hill, the sound of a voice carried on the wind drawing him closer.

He reached the top of the rise and peered down into a clearing, where an army had been gathered. They were angels, hundreds of angels garbed in armor polished to gleaming, and they stood unmoving, enraptured as they listened to one of their own. Clearly their leader, he paced before them, words of inspiration spilling from his mouth, and Aaron could see why they would have pledged their allegiance. There was something about him, a charisma that was impossible to deny.

As beautiful as the morning stars, he heard a voice whisper at the back of his mind, and he could not disagree.

And then the leader, the Morningstar, walked among his troops laying his hand upon each and every one of them, and as he touched them, bestowing upon them a special gift, weapons of fire sprang to life in their grasp, and they were ready to fight.

Ready for war.

Aaron experienced a sudden wave of vertigo, as if the world around him were being yanked away to be replaced by another time, another place, and he struggled to remain standing. He was on a battlefield now, surrounded by the unbridled carnage that was war. Soldiers he had watched rallied by the Morningstar were battling an army of equal savagery. He saw Camael and Verchiel fighting side by side against the Morningstar's army. The screams of the dying and the maimed filled the air as blazing swords hacked away limbs and snuffed out life, and angels fell helplessly from the sky, their wings consumed by flames of heavenly fire.

It was horrible; one of the most awesome yet disturbing sights he had ever seen. He wanted to turn away, to pull his eyes from the scenes of brutality, the broken and burning bodies of angels, the golden grass trampled, the ground stained with the dark blood of the heavenly. But it was everywhere; no matter where he looked, there was death.

Aaron's eyes were suddenly drawn to the Morningstar, his sword of fire hacking a swath through the opposing forces. His army was vanquished, but still he fought on, flaxen wings spread wide, slashing his way toward a tower made of glass, crystal maybe, that seemed to go up into the sky forever. The angel was screaming and there were tears on his face. Aaron could feel his sadness, for the sorrow that permeated the atmosphere of this place was so strong as to be nearly palpable.

The Morningstar screamed up at the crystalline tower, shaking his armored fist and demanding that He who sits on high come down to face him. And with wings beating air ripe with the smells of bloodshed, he began to ascend. The skies grew dark, thick with roiling clouds of gunmetal gray, and thunder rumbled ominously, causing the very environment to tremble. But the Morningstar continued to rise, flying steadily upward, sword of fire brandished in his grip, unhindered by the threat of storm.

Aaron could feel it before it actually happened, as if the air itself had become charged with electricity. He wanted to warn the beautiful soldier, but it was too late. A bolt of lightning resembling a long, gnarled finger, reached down from the gray, endless clouds and touched the warrior of Heaven. There was a flash of blinding light, and the Morningstar tumbled, burning, from the sky.

Stay down, Aaron whispered as he watched the figure twitch and then force himself to rise.

The Morningstar swayed upon legs charred black, and another blade of fire appeared in his hand. Again he looked up at the glass tower and raised his sword in defiance. *"How?"* he shrieked pitifully through a mouth now nothing more than a blackened hole. *"How can you love them more than us?"*

With wings still afire, he leaped back into the air, but his ascent was slower than before. The heavens growled with menace, as if displeased by his defiance, and birdlike shrieks filled the world. Aaron watched as the soldiers of the opposing army attacked the Morningstar, grabbing at his injured form, pulling him back to the ground, where they pitilessly set upon him with their weapons of fire.

He could feel the Morningstar's pain, every jab, every stab of the soldiers' searing blades, as if the attacks were being perpetrated upon him. Aaron fell to the ground, his eyes transfixed upon the violence before him, the blood of vanquished angels seeping through the knees of his pants.

Numbness had invaded his body, and he fought to stay conscious—to stay alive. But the darkness had him again in its grasp, and it pulled him below to a place where he could die in peace, the very same place that the angelic essence had resided before it had come awake on his eighteenth birthday. This was where he would slip from life, allowing the angelic power total mastery of his fragile human shell.

For a brief moment Aaron was convinced that this was the right thing for him to do. In this deep place of shadow there was no worry, no irritating mysteries of angelic powers, there was only comforting peace. Escape from the responsibilities heaped upon him by ancient prophecy.

"Aaron! He's hurting me!"

Aaron's tranquility was suddenly shattered by a cry for help, a desperate plea that echoed in the darkness. He tried to ignore it, but there was something about the voice that stirred within him a desire to live.

"Where are you, Aaron? He'll keep hurting me unless you come."

"Vilma," Aaron whispered within the constricting cocoon of shadow, and opened his eyes to a vision of the girl he believed he loved in the clutches of Verchiel. It was but a flash of sight, but it was enough to stir him from the comforting embrace of his impending death.

"Please! Aaron!"

The angelic essence fought to keep him submerged in the depths of oblivion, but Vilma needed him, Stevie and the fallen needed him, and he felt ashamed that he had even considered giving in. The closer he got to awareness, the more he felt the painful effects the poison had wrought upon his body, and he was reminded of, and inspired by, the Morningstar, burned black by the finger of God, but still he fought on.

Aaron came awake on his knees, now in the kitchen of Belphegor's home, his body wracked with bone-snapping convulsions. He pitched forward and vomited up the poison. Slowly he raised his head, wiping the remains of the revolting fluid that dribbled down his chin, to see Belphegor leaning forward on a wooden chair, offering him a white paper napkin.

"What did you see?" the angel asked, a gleam of excitement in his ancient eyes.

"Vilma." Aaron struggled to stand.

"Who?"

"I have to go to her," Aaron said, the familiar feeling of dread he'd been carrying since his life so dramatically changed replacing the nausea in his stomach.

"He has her. Verchiel has her."

chapter nine

"Vilma?" Belphegor asked, confused. "Who, may I ask, is Vilma?"

Aaron swayed upon legs that seemed to be made of rubber, grabbing hold of the kitchen doorframe to steady himself. "She's my girl . . ." He paused, rethinking his answer. "She's somebody from my old life, someone very important to me—and Verchiel has her." Images of the screaming girl flashed across his vision. He could hear her calling out to him.

"He is attempting to get to you through your friends," Belphegor commented matter-of-factly. "Typical behavior for one such as he."

Aaron didn't understand. Somehow Vilma had reached out and touched his mind.

But how?

"What did you see when you went inside,

Aaron?" Belphegor questioned. "You must tell me everything—"

Aaron raised a hand to interrupt him. "She was inside my head." He stared hard at Belphegor. "How is that possible, unless? . . ."

Belphegor slowly nodded, sensing that Aaron already suspected the answer. "Unless she is as you are," he finished.

It hit Aaron like a physical blow and he fell back against the doorframe, sliding to the floor as his knees gave out. "I can't believe it," he muttered in amazement. He remembered every moment, however brief, he had shared with her. There was no doubt of the attraction, but evidently the reason went far beyond raging hormones. They were of the same kind.

Nephilim.

"Just when I think I've seen it all," he said with an exasperated shake of his head.

Belphegor left the table and moved to Aaron's side. He seemed impatient, anxious. "Never mind your friend," he said. "What did you *see*, Aaron?"

"I don't have time for this," Aaron said, climbing to his feet. "She needs me."

Belphegor reached out and grabbed hold of his arm in a powerful grip. "I need to know what you saw," he stressed. "The people of Aerie need to know what you saw."

Aaron shook off the old angel's grasp. "I saw

an angel—and he was one of the most beautiful things I have ever seen," he said, not without a little embarrassment, especially as he caught the look on Belphegor's face. "It's not sexual or anything," he explained. "It was just the way he carried himself. I could feel the devotion of his army in the air. I could feel how much they loved him."

"You . . . you saw the Morningstar?" Belphegor stammered, as if he were afraid of something.

Aaron nodded, a bit taken aback by the old angel's reaction. "And there was a battle," he said, the violent, disturbing imagery forever burned into his psyche. "It was horrible," he added. "And incredibly sad."

Belphegor stared off into space, thoughtfully stroking his chin.

"What does it mean, Belphegor?" Aaron asked cautiously. "What does all of this have to do with me?"

The old fallen slowly refocused his gaze on Aaron. "The pain and the sadness, the death and the violence—I believe that is the power from which you were born."

Aaron shook his head. "I don't understand."

"But you will," Belphegor said with authority. "We shall go to Scholar, and together we'll delve deeper into the mystery of your origin—"

"No," Aaron said emphatically. "You don't understand. Vilma is in trouble and I have to go to her." Aaron moved past the old angel, his resolve lending new strength to his legs. "I can't afford to waste any more time."

He had pulled open the kitchen door and was ready to step outside when Belphegor again grabbed him.

"We're close, Aaron," he said.

There was a tension in his voice that hadn't been there before, a veiled excitement hinting that the angel knew more than he was letting on. It almost drew Aaron back, but then he remembered Vilma's face—her beautiful face, twisted in pain and fear—and he knew he had no choice.

He shrugged Belphegor's hand away and started down the stairs. "I'm sorry, but I have to go," he said over his shoulder. "I'll come back just as soon as—"

Lehash stood in the street just outside the yard. A long, thin cigar dangled at the corner of his mouth, the smoke trailing from its tip forming a misty halo around his head. "Is there a problem, boy?" he asked in a grave voice, the cigar bobbing up and down like a conductor's baton as he spoke.

Aaron shook his head, fully feeling the menace that radiated from the Aerie constable. "Not yet," he answered, trying to keep the fear from his voice.

Belphegor came up behind him. "It's all right, Lehash," he said reassuringly. "Come back inside, Aaron. We'll talk."

"I'm going," Aaron said defiantly, and began to push past them.

Lehash came forward, and Aaron saw the shimmer of fire in his hands that signaled the arrival of his golden weapons. "I'd listen to the boss if I was you," he said with a threatening hiss, blocking Aaron's path.

"It could be a trap, Aaron," Belphegor cautioned behind him. "Verchiel could be using your friend to strike, not only at you, but at us, at Aerie. I'm sorry, but we can't let you go, there's far too much at stake."

Lehash brandished his guns menacingly. "You heard 'im," he said, motioning for Aaron to return to the house. "Get back in there before things get serious."

"They already have," Aaron said, feeling the power come alive within him. It was like the world's biggest head rush, and he braced himself, not even trying to hold back its coming.

A crowd of citizens had started to gather, coming out of their decrepit homes as if drawn by the potential for violence. Aaron could see their nervous glances, hear their whispering.

"I knew he'd be trouble." "Him? He's not the One—I can't believe anyone could be so foolish as to think that." "Lehash will put him in his place."

The sigils emerged on Aaron's flesh, and he let his wings of solid black unfold. He heard gasps from the gathered, and even Lehash seemed genuinely taken aback as Aaron stepped past the constable and into the street. The citizens were in awe. He could see it in their eyes— or maybe it was something else they were seeing, he decided, as he heard the sharp click of twin gun hammers being pulled back from behind.

Aaron reacted purely on instinct; there was no inner struggle, no attempt to keep the power at bay, he simply let it flow through him, guiding its might with a tempered hand. He spun around to face his potential foe, a feral snarl upon his lips. With a thunderous clap of sound, one of the gunslinger's pistols belched fire made solid, and it hurtled across the short expanse to burrow beneath the soft flesh of the Nephilim's shoulder.

Aaron fell backward, a scream upon his lips as he hit the street, his mighty wings cushioning the fall. The pain was bad, and his left side was growing numb as he lay gazing up at the early morning sky. Aaron knew that he should get up—for Stevie's sake, for Vilma's—but he wasn't sure he had the strength to do so.

The citizens' murmurs sounded to him like a swarm of bees roused to anger by a threat to their hive. Lehash stood over him, smoking pistol still in his grasp. There was cruelty in his steely gaze, a look that said so much more than words.

"Look at you," he said in a whisper meant

only for Aaron's ears. "Can't even save yourself, never mind us." The gunslinger stared down his arm, down the length of his golden weapon. "How dare you fill their hearts with hope and then rip it away. Haven't we suffered enough without the likes of you?" Lehash came closer. "I should kill you now."

Aaron lay still, his gaze locked on the barrel of the pistol that hovered above him ominously like a black, unblinking eye. Lehash's finger twitched upon the trigger, and the Nephilim's mind was assaulted with the brutal images of war. He again saw the Morningstar walking among his troops, laying his hand upon them, giving something of himself to each and every one. And he witnessed them in battle, fighting for their master's cause—dying for their master's cause—and he was filled with their purpose, with their power and strength.

The sigils on his body suddenly burned as if painted with acid, and Aaron sprang up from the street, a cry of rage from somewhere deep inside escaping his lips. The gunslinger fired, but this time the bullet did not find its target. Aaron lashed out with one of his wings, swatting the weapon from the constable's grasp. "No more guns," he commanded, grabbing the fallen angel's wrist and violently twisting his arm so that he dropped the second of the golden guns.

Aaron looked into the constable's eyes and saw that something new had taken the place of steely cruelty. He saw the beginnings of fear, but he did not want that. Effortlessly he hurled Lehash away. All he wanted was to save the people he loved.

Lehash landed in the street about six feet away, scattering citizens that had gathered there. A hush had fallen over the crowd, and they watched him in pregnant silence. Belphegor came forward to help Lehash as sparks danced in the constable's hands. Aaron tensed, a weapon of his own ready to surge to life.

"No," Belphegor commanded in a powerful voice.

Lehash stared at his superior, confusion on his grizzled face.

"Let him go."

Lehash's eyes went wide in shock. "You can't do this," he sputtered. "He'll bring Verchiel and his bloodthirsty rabble down on our heads for sure!"

Belphegor raised a hand and closed his eyes. "You heard me, let the boy go."

From across the street Aaron met Belphegor's eyes and a jolt like electricity passed through his body.

"If you're going to go," Belphegor said, "then go now."

Aaron found it difficult to look away from the angel's intense gaze. *Am I doing the right thing?* he fretted. Doubt crept into his thoughts, but then images of Vilma and the still-missing

Stevie filled his mind, and it didn't matter anymore if it was right or wrong. He had to go. "I'll come back," he said as he spread his wings.

"I hope you do," Belphegor replied, a scowling Lehash at his side.

Aaron took one final look about Aerie and saw Camael, Gabriel, and Lorelei heading toward him. He wanted to tell them what he was doing—what he had to do—but he didn't want to stop, unsure if he would have the courage to recommence if he did. They would have to understand.

The image of his destination fresh inside his head, Aaron folded his wings about himself and was gone.

"Maybe he didn't see us," Gabriel said forlornly.

But Camael knew differently. He had looked into the boy's eyes before he departed.

The fallen angel had known that it was only a matter of time before the violence in his life again reared its ugly head and his brief respite would end. It had been pleasurable while it lasted.

"What's going on?" Lorelei was asking an older woman whom Camael recognized as Marjorie. He had saved her from one of Verchiel's hunting parties sometime in the 1950s, and she still bore a red, ragged scar upon her cheek to commemorate the Powers' ruthless attack.

The woman wrung her hands nervously, staring off in the direction from which Aaron had departed. "He's gone," she said, her voice filled with concern. "There was a fight, and then he left us." Marjorie looked past Lorelei to Camael. "Is he coming back?" she asked pleadingly. "Can you tell me if the Chosen One is coming back?"

Lorelei turned to him as well, as though he might have some special insight into the situation unfolding.

"Let us find Belphegor," Camael said, ignoring the women's plaintive questions, and continuing down the street, Gabriel close at his heels.

The citizens of Aerie were abuzz, and as he passed, their eyes caught his, frantic for answers to assuage their fears. A hand shot out to grip his arm and Camael stared into the face of Scholar. He believed his true name to be Tumael, once a member of the host called Principalities. He was wild eyed, as anxious as the others around him.

"Do you know where he's gone—the boy?" Tumael asked nervously, his grip tight with desperation. "We have to get him back . . . we . . . we can't let him walk away from us, Camael. Do you understand the importance of what I'm saying?"

Camael knew exactly, but until he found out what had happened, he could offer no words of solace. "Belphegor. I need to speak with him."

The fallen angel pointed toward a house not far from where they stood.

"Come, Gabriel," Camael said to the dog that waited obediently by his side.

They approached the home, catching sight of Lorelei disappearing into the backyard. As they rounded the corner of the house, they were met by voices raised in panicked fury. Lehash and his daughter were in the midst of a heated argument, arms flailing as they railed against each other. Belphegor was across the yard, removed from the commotion, examining the branches of a young sapling.

"Why don't you go and talk with Belphegor," Camael told the Labrador at his side. "Maybe he can tell you where Aaron has gone."

Tail wagging, Gabriel trotted toward Aerie's Founder, while Camael turned his attention to the angry constable.

"You," Lehash growled, raising an accusatory hand as Camael approached. "This is your fault!"

"Lehash, stop," Lorelei pleaded.

"Would anyone care to tell me what has happened?" Camael asked, carefully watching Lehash's hands for signs of his golden weaponry.

"Your Nephilim will be the death of us all," the constable spat, fists clenched in barely suppressed rage. "Filling all their heads with foolishness . . . we'll see how much of a messiah they think he is when we have Verchiel's soldiers breathing down our necks."

"Dad, please," Lorelei said, again trying to calm him. She touched the sleeve of his coat, but he pulled away roughly.

"Is that what this is really about, Lehash?" Camael asked. "Your lack of belief?"

Lehash scowled. "Don't matter what I believe," he said with a sorrowful shake of his head. He glanced over at Belphegor and Gabriel. "Don't matter what any of us believes. Verchiel will have what he's been waiting for—a good whiff of Aerie, and that's all the son of a bitch will need to destroy us."

"Where has Aaron gone?"

"To rescue a friend—a female—from Verchiel," Lehash explained. He smiled, but the expression was void of any humor. "With the scent of where he's been these last weeks clinging to him like cheap perfume. Should have just handed a map to the Powers, get the slaughter over with all the quicker."

The fallen angel pushed past, his piece said, Lorelei close behind. Her eyes briefly touched Camael's. "I'm sorry," she said, and he wondered if she was apologizing for her father's behavior, or perhaps giving her condolences for what they believed to be Aerie's inevitable demise.

Camael joined Belphegor, who was leaning down to pet Gabriel.

"Aaron's gone to find Vilma," the dog said, tipping his head back so the old angel would scratch beneath his throat. "She's the one he talks to on the computer sometimes."

"I believe that she, too, is a Nephilim." Belphegor spoke as he obliged the animal's wants. "Her angelic nature cried out to him as he was exploring his own." He stopped patting Gabriel, much to the dog's disappointment, and turned his attention to Camael. "Verchiel has her." He looked out to the neighborhood beyond the yard. "It's truly amazing how quickly things change, Camael," Belphegor said with a wistful smile. "You never really see it coming; it's just suddenly there, the eye of the speeding locomotive bearing down upon you."

"You could have stopped him," Camael said. "Or you could have found me and I would have—"

Again Belphegor smiled sadly. "It doesn't really matter that he's gone." He began to stroll from the yard, Gabriel and Camael following at his side. "Change is coming to Aerie, and whether it be the machinations of prophecy, or just plain fate, there's nothing we can do to stop it."

Aerie's citizens were still milling about the street, their gazes haunted.

"They can sense it as much as you and I," Belphegor said, gesturing at the crowd.

He stopped in the middle of the street and closed his eyes. With a soft grunt of exertion, his wings sprang from his back, sad-looking things of dingy gray and missing feathers. "Join me for a moment," he said, motioning for Camael to follow as he launched himself into the air, the wings, surprisingly, having the strength to lift him.

"Wait for me here," Camael told Gabriel, his own mighty wings sweeping from his back and taking him heavenward.

Like I have a choice, he heard the dog mumble as he ascended.

It was early morning, the sun just starting to rise above the horizon, illuminating the dilapidated neighborhood below.

"Take a good long look, Camael," Belphegor said, gesticulating with a hand to Aerie beneath him as his wings pounded the air. "For soon, it's all going to change."

Camael looked below, at the run-down houses, the cracked and untended streets, the high barbed-wire fence that encircled it, and felt the pangs of something he had not experienced since he first left heavenly paradise on a mission of murder. He had not had a home—a true place of belonging—in countless millenia. The troubling thought of losing this one filled him with great sorrow.

And then, hovering above the neighborhood, the former leader of the Powers suddenly knew what was required of him. It was his way of giving thanks to those who had accepted him into their community, despite his loathsome past.

Camael would do everything within his strength to see that Aerie lived on, and may Heaven have pity on any who dared try to keep him from his task.

† † †

Aaron had recognized Vilma's location in the vision almost immediately: the red metal lockers, the cracked plaster walls painted eggshell white, a handmade poster that should have been taken down months ago asking for canned donations for a Thanksgiving food drive. He opened his wings to an empty parking lot, for it was still quite early in the morning, and gazed at Kenneth Curtis High School. A pang of nostalgia spread through him; memories, both good and bad, flooded his thoughts.

As he crossed the lot to the redbrick-and-concrete building, his wings receded and the fearsome marks upon his flesh faded. As an afterthought, he willed himself invisible, not wanting an early riser to see him going into the building, and call the police. He climbed the steps leading to the large, double doors, thinking of how much his life had changed in such a brief amount of time. A little over a month ago he had been a student here, a senior, preparing to graduate and begin the next phase of his life. *The next phase happened all right, but not how I would have planned it.* He reached the top of the stairs and pulled on one of the doors. It was unlocked and his flesh tingled with the sensation of caution.

The smells of the old building wafted out to greet him. He remembered his first day at Ken Curtis. He hadn't wanted to return for a second, but he did, and each day he went back, it got a little easier. He also recalled the first day he had seen Vilma, and with that recollection came the realization of how much was now at stake.

He stepped into the school, and the door closed gradually behind him. Ahead, standing near the doorway of the principal's office, stood an angel. He was clothed as Aaron had come to expect: dark suit, trench coat—as if he'd just come from a funeral—and in his hand he held a flaming sword.

Expecting a fight, Aaron created a weapon of his own and felt the strange symbols return to his flesh. It was amazing how easily the transformation came now. *Maybe I'm finally getting the hang of this thing,* he thought absently.

Instead of brandishing his weapon, the Powers' soldier turned away and approached a set of swinging doors. With his free hand he pushed one side open and bowed his head.

Aaron cautiously proceeded down the hallway toward the doors, the angel watching, quelled anger in his dark eyes. But he remained silent, still holding the door for him. Aaron strode through defiantly. He could feel the angel's stare upon his back, cold and murderous, but did not give him the satisfaction of turning to meet his gaze. More angels emerged from the classrooms along the hall, motioning with a flourish of their flaming blades for him to proceed past them.

At the top of the stairs leading down into the basement, another angel waited and gestured for him to descend. Of course he had to descend; his brain raced. Wasn't that one of the first things he had learned in freshman English? That the protagonist must always descend to confront what plagues him before his victory and eventual ascension.

As with the others in the corridor behind him, the angel warrior at the stairs said nothing as he passed. Aaron went down the steps to the first landing and chanced a look back. The angel was watching him, a cruel smile on its thin, bloodless lips. "Catch you on the way back," Aaron called. He had no idea what the Powers had in store for him below, but he wasn't about to give them the satisfaction of believing he was afraid.

He continued down into the basement, the illumination thrown by his flaming blade lighting the way. The air below was thick with the smell of chlorine, and at the foot of the stairs he stopped, trying to decide if he should head toward the school's pool or the gymnasium.

It didn't take long for another of Verchiel's soldiers to appear and motion him toward the gym. Aaron had never particularly enjoyed phys ed, and found it strangely fitting that the Powers would summon him there. His teacher had been a jock from way back and didn't much care for anyone who wasn't on the football team. "Abandon hope all ye who enter," the Nephilim muttered as he walked through the door and into the gymnasium, the strange and disturbing vision of angels playing a game of shirts-versus-skins basketball running through his head.

But those images were soon dispelled. The room was dark, red exit signs and the swords of the angelic army that awaited him providing the only light. Aaron felt his heart sink, even with the essence inside him. *How can I ever hope to fight so many?* They were everywhere: on the bleachers, perched atop the basketball rims, and up above in the girder-latticed ceiling. They reminded him of pigeons, only these birds were far more dangerous.

"We've been waiting for you," said a voice that made his flesh tingle as if covered with ants.

Immediately Aaron felt the wings on his back begin to stir. On cue, a group of angels atop the bleachers stepped aside to reveal Verchiel. He was reclining in the wooden seats, as if watching a game, the unconscious Vilma lying beside him. Aaron was disappointed to see that Stevie was not there as well. His pulse quickened as his wings sprang from his back. *This is it,* he thought, and the power inside him writhed in anticipation. The Powers' leader watched him with eyes like shiny black marbles, and Aaron noticed that the angel's face still bore the angry scars from their first confrontation back in Lynn.

"Let her go, Verchiel," he said, raising his

blade of fire. "She's done nothing to you. It's me that you want."

The Powers' leader gazed with disgust at the unconscious young woman. "That is where you are wrong, animal," he said in a voice filled with contempt. "My problem has grown far larger than you." He touched Vilma then, a gentle caress with fingertips that glowed like white-hot metal, and she cried out in pain.

Aaron surged forward, wings spread wide to lift him into the air, but something moved in the periphery of his sight, something that was beside him before his brain even had a chance to react. It lashed out at him, a gauntlet of metal connecting with the side of his face, sending him crashing to the slick wooden floor in a heap.

"What you are, what you represent, is a virulent disease," Verchiel said from the bleachers above, "a disease that has infected this world."

Aaron's head was ringing and he was finding it difficult to focus. But the power of the Nephilim coursed through his body, urging him to his feet. Sensing his attacker close by, Aaron lashed out with his sword of flame. The blade touched nothing.

"But I believe I have found a cure for this epidemic." Aaron could hear Verchiel descending the wooden bleachers a step at a time.

Another blow fell on the back of his neck with such force that he wondered if it had been broken. He rolled onto his back and gazed up into the fearsome visage of a warrior clad entirely in armor of red—the color of spilled blood.

"This is Malak," he heard Verchiel say from somewhere nearby. "And he will be your death, body and spirit."

And as Aaron studied the armored figure looming menacingly above him, he had a sneaking suspicion that Verchiel might very well be right.

chapter ten

The armored warrior called Malak reached into the air, and from some hidden pocket in space, removed a sword of dark metal. The light of the Powers' flaming weapons illuminated strange etchings on the blade, similar to those on the manacles Aaron had worn in Aerie. But he had little time to consider that, as Malak brought the weapon down, intending to cleave his skull in two.

Aaron rolled to the side, then flexing his powerful wings, propelled himself upward and lashed out with his own sword. The burning blade clipped Malak's shoulder, sending a shower of sparks into the air. Malak was already moving to counter the attack, his sword gone, replaced with a long spear made of the same dark, etched metal. He struck out with the shaft of the spear, catching Aaron on the chin. The

Nephilim stumbled to the side and watched from the corner of his eye as the armored warrior lunged forward, the spear's tip searching for something vital.

His actions almost reflex, Aaron swatted the spearhead away with his sword of fire, severing it from the body of the shaft. He spun around, the weapon in his hand now seeking Malak's heart, momentarily amazed by the fluidity of his thoughts and movements. No longer did he feel the struggle inside him between what was angelic and what was human. But now wasn't the time for reflection.

Malak had dropped what was left of his spear and grabbed hold of Aaron's fiery blade, halting its deadly progress less than a half inch from his ornate chest plate. Aaron bore down upon the blade with all his might, but Malak's strength was incredible, his armored hand glowing white hot with the heat of heavenly fire. Suddenly there was a blinding flash, and the combatants were thrown apart by the force of the powerful concussion. Aaron shook away the cotton that seemed to fill his head, coming to a disturbing realization: Malak had broken his blade. The warrior had actually destroyed his sword of fire. He quickly scrambled to his feet. Malak was already standing, flexing the hand that had held back Aaron's sword of fire. The armored glove had already cooled, returning to its original color of ore.

A strange sound filled the air. Malak was laughing—a high-pitched titter that reminded Aaron more of a small child amused by cartoon antics on television than the laugh of a blood-thirsty warrior. Then, as abruptly as it had be-gun, Malak's laughter ended, and where there had been nothing in his armored hand, there were suddenly razor-sharp throwing stars. Aaron heard their metal surfaces grinding together as Malak bent forward and let the blades fly. He spread his wings and took to the air, the stars finding targets instead in the bodies of the Powers' angels that were unlucky enough to be standing nearby watching the conflict unfold.

He glided backward, keeping a cautious eye on the armored warrior already on the move. Not paying attention to his surroundings, his back hit up against something solid and in-stinctively a sword grew in his hand. He spun, hacking at what was behind him. Angels scat-tered in a flutter of wings and trench coats, hissing menacingly, as Aaron's blade passed through the steel poles of a basketball hoop, sending the backboard crashing to the gymna-sium floor.

Distracted, Aaron didn't notice Malak until it was too late. The armored warrior tossed a net made of thin, flexible strands of the same black metal as his weapons and ensnared the Nephilim. The weighted ends of the net restricted Aaron's wings, and he fell to the floor atop the downed backboard. Eager to vanquish his prey, Malak charged; a dagger caked with the blood of earlier kills clutched in his armored hand.

Aaron concentrated on a new weapon, and another sword came to be in his grasp, melting through the tight weave of the net. But before he could free himself completely, Malak was upon him. He tried to turn away, but his movement was hindered by the net and the weight of his armored assailant, and the dagger's blade bit deep into his already wounded shoulder. Aaron cried out, thrashing violently beneath Malak's attack and managing to knock him to one side. With his sword of fire, he sliced upward through the metal mesh, cutting an opening big enough to crawl through.

As he sloughed off the net Aaron watched with muted horror: His armored attacker brought the knife blade to the face of his helmet, the tip of a pink tongue snaked from the mask and licked the Nephilim's blood from the weapon's edge. For an instant he wondered what kind of creature resided behind the concealing helmet of scarlet, recalling Camael's haunting explanation of the Powers' use of the handicapped. He thought of his foster brother, steeling his resolve against his foe and the others he would eventually have to face. Though his shoulder burned as if on fire, Aaron held his sword tightly and slowly pointed the fiery blade across the gym where his opponent waited.

"You," Aaron said in a booming voice filled with authority. "Let's finish this."

Malak giggled again. His knife disappeared and he withdrew a double-bladed battle-ax from the air to replace it. The warrior hefted the heavy weapon in one hand. "Bootiful," he said through his mask of red metal.

Bootiful.

The word hit him like one of Lehash's flaming bullets, and Aaron lowered his weapon in shock.

"What did you say?" he asked the scarlet-garbed warrior.

Again Malak giggled, that high-pitched titter that put his nerves on edge.

"What's the matter, Nephilim?" he heard Verchiel ask with mock concern.

Aaron chanced a glance at the heavenly monster. He was standing before the bleachers, hands clasped behind his back, a throng of angel soldiers surrounding him. One of them had Vilma slung over its shoulder, as if she were nothing more than an afterthought.

"Has something plucked a chord of familiarity?"

Malak was suddenly before him, swinging the blade of his double-headed ax. Aaron sprang back from the vicious blade, studying his attacker's movement, the single word still echoing dangerously in his head.

Bootiful.

The ax buried itself deep into the shiny, hardwood floor, but Malak quickly retrieved it, coming at him again. The warrior swung his weapon of war, and this time Aaron responded in kind, deflecting the ax with his sword of fire.

"Why did you say that word?" he hissed, launching his own assault against Malak.

The warrior giggled, childlike, as he ducked beneath the swipe of Aaron's blade.

"Why did you say it?" he shouted frantically, an idea almost too horrible for him to comprehend beginning to form in his mind. His attack upon the Powers' assassin grew wilder, driving Malak back across the gym.

Malak countered as fast as Aaron struck, blocking and avoiding the weapon of heavenly fire with ease.

Verchiel was laughing, a grating sound, like the cawing of some carrion bird.

Aaron hacked downward with all his might, but Malak stepped aside, bringing his armored foot down upon the blade, trapping it against the floor as he lashed out with his ax. Aaron felt the bite of the razor-sharp blade as it cut through the fabric of his shirt and the skin beneath. He jumped back, leaving his pinned sword to disperse in a flash. Slowly he lowered his hand to his stomach, then brought it up to his face. His fingertips were stained the color of his attacker's armor.

The sight of his own blood and the unsettling sound of Verchiel's laughter served only to inflame his rage. He felt the power of the Nephilim inside him and it coursed through his muscles—through the entire fiber of his being. If he were to survive this conflict, he had to trust the warrior's nature he had inherited. He had to defeat this armored foe, but still he could not get past the implication of Verchiel's words.

Has something plucked a chord of familiarity?

Malak came at him again, battle-ax at the ready, and Aaron sprang forward to meet the attack. He dove low, connecting with the warrior's armor-plated legs, and they crashed to the floor in a thrashing pile. Malak held on to his ax and tried to use it to drive his opponent from atop him, but Aaron kept close, rendering the weapon useless. The power of the Nephilim shrieked a cry of battle, and Aaron found himself caught up in a wave of might that flooded his body, his every sense. *This must be what Camael was talking about, the unification of the human and the angelic.* It was wonderful, and for the first time since learning of his angelic heritage, Aaron Corbet felt truly complete.

He fought to his feet and wrenched the battle-ax from Malak's grasp.

"This is over," he growled, looming over the armored warrior, ax in hand, glaring at Verchiel and his followers around the gym. The sigils upon his body pulsed with a life all their own, and he spread his wings to their full span. *What a sight I must be*, he thought, inundated by feelings of perfection.

"Yes, you are right," Verchiel agreed with a casual nod. "I tire of these games. Malak, show your face."

Aaron almost screamed for the warrior to stop, not wanting to see what he already suspected. Malak reached up and yanked the scarlet helmet from his head.

"Do you see who you have been fighting, Nephilim?" Verchiel asked, moving closer with his angelic throng.

"No," Aaron cried, unable to tear his gaze away from the familiar features of the young man lying before him. He did not know this person, but then again, he did. "You son of bitch, what have you done?"

"With the magick of the Archons, we have transformed what by human standards was considered limited in its usefulness, into a precision weapon."

Malak looked up at Aaron with eyes that once held the innocence of a special child, but now were filled with something else, something deadly. These eyes told a story of death; they were the eyes of a killer. The revelation was even worse than he'd imagined.

The ax slipped from Aaron's hands and clattered upon the floor. "Stevie?" he asked in a trembling whisper, giving credence to what should have been impossible. He willed away the sigils and his formidable wings. "It's me," he said, touching his chest with a trembling, blood-stained hand. Images of a past that seemed thousands of years ago, of the autistic child as he should have been, flashed through Aaron's mind. "It's me—it's Aaron," he said, offering the young man his hand.

At first there was nothing that showed even the slightest hint of humanity in the gaze that met Aaron's. It was like looking into the eyes of a wild animal, but then there came a spark and Malak's eyes twinkled with recognition.

"Aaron?" Stevie asked in a voice very much like that of a child, and his armored hand took hold of his brother's.

Every instinct screamed for Aaron to pull away. "Stevie," he began.

The warrior in red shook his head crazily from side to side, an idiot's grin spreading across his dull features. "Not Stevie," he said as Aaron watched him reach into a pocket of air with his free hand and withdraw a fearsome medieval mace. "Malak!" he shouted, and bludgeoned Aaron across the face with its studded head before the Nephilim had an opportunity to react.

Aaron fell to the floor, the world spinning and his every sense scrambled. He shook his head and slowly rose to his knees, the smell of his own blood wafting up into his nostrils. His scalp was bleeding. As his vision cleared, he could see that Verchiel and his soldiers were standing in a circle around them. The room was eerily quiet, the only sound the armored footfalls of Malak's approach. Aaron summoned another sword of fire.

He gazed into the face of his little brother, his murderous countenance filling the Nephilim with an overwhelming despair. He didn't want to think about what the Powers had done to the child, did not want to know the horror and pain his little brother had endured. But he felt the guilt of not being there to protect him from harm just the same.

Halfheartedly, he raised his weapon of heavenly flame. "I . . . I don't want to do this," he said.

Malak responded with a horrible smile, and Aaron was reminded of a raccoon with rabies that had once been brought to the veterinary hospital where he used to work. Nothing could be done for the animal, and with a heavy heart, he realized the same was true now.

"I'm so sorry," he whispered as Malak rushed toward him, mace raised to strike. Aaron deflected the blow, but hesitated in his own attack. The warrior swung again, and this time the mace connected with Aaron's injured shoulder. He cried out and tried to back away, but came up against a living wall of Powers' soldiers.

"It ends here, Nephilim," Verchiel barked

from across the circle. "It's time to remove from this world the sickness you represent." The Powers' commander looked to the unconscious Vilma, draped over the shoulder of the angel standing beside him, and sneered as he reached out to touch her raven black hair. "Let us hope it can survive the cleansing."

Aaron's arm throbbed with every staccato beat of his heart, and he was finding it difficult to hold on to his sword. The niggling idea that perhaps he should have listened to Belphegor played at the corner of his thoughts, but it was too late now for second guesses. He had already failed his brother; he wasn't about to fail Vilma as well.

Verchiel's emotionless black eyes fell upon his champion. "Kill the abomination and be done with it," he ordered.

Malak charged at Aaron, weapon raised, his features twisted in bloodlust. They were about to continue their dance of battle, when the gymnasium was suddenly filled with the sound of a booming voice.

"The Nephilim is under my protection."

Malak's attack came to a screeching halt, and the Powers searched for the source of the authoritative proclamation. The angels' circle broke to reveal the striking figure of Camael standing in the gymnasium doorway, Gabriel attentively at his side.

"And mine too," said the dog in a throaty growl.

"Then it is only fitting that you all die together," Verchiel said, a sword igniting in his hand.

Everything became incredibly still, a tension so thick in the air that it seemed to have substance. And then Vilma began to scream, an anguished wail of terror that alluded to the violence that was yet to come.

Still slung over the shoulder of a Powers' soldier, Vilma Santiago had come noisily awake. Her scream was bloodcurdling, born out of sheer terror, and Aaron's heart nearly broke in sympathy. But he had little time to consider her fear, for her cry had acted as a kind of starter's pistol, signaling the beginning of an inevitable conflict.

The Powers were the first to react. With birdlike squawks, they leaped into the air, wings pounding, weapons of fire clenched in their hands. Camael reacted in kind, propelling himself up to confront his attackers above the gym floor.

Malak turned to Aaron, a malicious grin gracing his pale features. He began to lift the mace, but this time, Aaron was faster. He brought forth his wings, and as the mighty appendages unfurled, the body of his right wing caught his attacker, swatting him aside. Through the chaos, Aaron set his sights on Vilma, who was thrashing wildly in the clutches of her angelic keeper. Desperately trying to ignore the throbbing pain in his head and shoulder, he began to make his way toward the girl and her captor, carefully avoiding the burning bodies of angels as they fell from the air, victims of Camael's battle prowess.

From the corner of his eye, Aaron glimpsed movement and turned just in time to avoid the blade of a broadsword as it attempted to split his skull. He stared into the still-grinning face of Malak. The armored warrior was already bringing the enormous sword around for another strike, but Aaron brought his own blade up to counter the attack before it could cut him in two. Malak stepped in close and drove a metal-clad knee up into the Nephilim's ribs. Aaron cried out in pain, but responded in kind, throwing an elbow into the bridge of Malak's nose.

The warrior of the Powers stumbled back, blood gushing from his nostrils. He brought his gloved hand to his nose and stared dumbfounded at the blood, and then Malak began to laugh. He plunged both hands into his magickal arsenal and emerged with two curved blades of Middle Eastern origin. "Pretty," he said through a spray of blood dripping from his nose. He brandished the unusual weapons and came toward Aaron again, his level of ferociousness seemingly endless.

Suddenly there was a rumbling growl, and a yellow blur moved between Aaron and his attacker. He watched stunned as Malak took the full weight of Gabriel's pounce and was knocked backward to the gym floor.

"Save Vilma," the dog barked, slamming the top of his thick skull down into the forehead of the Powers' assassin.

Across the gym floor littered with angelic dead, Aaron could see Vilma struggling with her captor. The Powers' angel was holding her wrist in one hand, while in the other was a dagger of flame. Aaron darted forward, but froze as the fearsome visage of Verchiel crossed his path.

"I've not forgotten you, animal," he snarled, the mottled scars on his once flawless features beaming a ruddy red. Like some great prehistoric bird, Verchiel opened his wings to their fullest and advanced. "I rather like the idea of killing you myself," he said with a predatory grin.

Aaron glanced quickly toward Vilma and back to his newest adversary. Taking a combat stance, he held his heavenly weapon high. "Let's do it then," he said, determined that nothing would keep him from the girl.

Then, as if Heaven had decided to answer his prayers, an angel fell from above, its body engulfed in flames. It landed atop Verchiel, knocking him to the ground. Aaron looked up to see Camael hovering above him, his suit tattered and torn, his exposed skin spattered with the blood of the vanquished. "Save the girl!" he ordered, before turning to defend himself against another wave of Powers' soldiers.

Vilma's captor had driven her to the floor, a fiery blade beginning to take form dangerously close to the delicate flesh of her throat. There was murder in the angel's face, and Aaron knew there was a chance that he would not reach her in time. But the image of a weapon took form in his mind—and a spear made from the heavenly fire that lived inside him became a thing of reality. Solid in his hand, he let the weapon fly and watched with great satisfaction as the razor-sharp tip plunged into the neck of the Powers' angel, knocking him away from the struggling girl and pinning his thrashing body to the bleachers.

Aaron was on the move again. "Vilma!" he shouted. The girl was in shock, stumbling about as she gazed around at the nightmarish visions unfolding before her. He called her name again, and she turned to look in his direction with fear-filled eyes.

He stopped before her and held out his hands. "It's me," he said in his most soothing voice. She stared at him, an expression of surprise gradually creeping across her features. He was pretty sure that at the moment he didn't look like the boy she'd said good-bye to in the hallway of Kenneth Curtis High School a few weeks ago, but now was not the time for explanations, all he cared about was keeping her alive. "It's Aaron," he continued, slowly reaching for her.

Vilma blinked, then turned and made a run for the door. Aaron dove for her, his powerful wings allowing him to glide the short distance and take her into his arms. "Please," he said, holding her tightly. "Listen to me."

She fought, punching, screaming, and kicking. She turned in his embrace and began to pound his chest with her fists. "No! No! No!"

"Vilma, it's really me," Aaron said in her native Portuguese. *"I've come to help you."*

For an instant she stopped fighting, looking into his eyes as if searching for lies in his words.

"Please, Vilma," he said again. *"You have to trust me."*

She sagged in his arms, the fight draining out of her. "I want to wake up," she said in a voice groggy with shock. "Just let me wake—"

There was an explosion from the center of the gymnasium, and Verchiel emerged from the conflagration, face twisted in madness as smoldering body parts of soldiers once in his service rained down around him.

"Aaron," Camael cried from above as he pitched another victim of his flaming swordplay at the Powers' commander. "Take the girl and leave!"

Gabriel charged across the gym. *"Yeah, let's get out of here."*

The yellow fur of the dog's face was spattered with blood, and Aaron wondered what it had taken to keep the armored Malak down. He gazed upward looking for Camael. The number of Powers' soldiers had diminished to five and still the warrior that he had learned to call friend fought on. "Camael!" he cried, Vilma slumped in his arms, his dog at his side. He gestured wildly for the angel to join them.

"Leave me!" the former leader of the Powers shouted as he swung his sword in a blazing arc, dispatching two more attackers.

"Nephilim!" Verchiel screamed as he strode across the bodies of his soldiers.

If they were going to leave together, it had to be now. Aaron again gazed up at his mentor. "Camael, please."

"Get out of here now," Camael commanded. "Too much depends upon your survival. Go. Now!" Then he spread his wings and hurled himself at Verchiel.

Aaron wanted to stay, but as he looked at the trembling girl in his arms, the realization of Camael's words slowly sank in. The citizens of Aerie were depending on him, and if he was indeed the Chosen One, he owed it to them to make their prophecy a reality. As much as it pained him, he knew that Camael was right. He had to leave.

"*Aaron, we should go,*" Gabriel said from his side, his warm body tightly pressed against his leg.

"I think you're right," Aaron answered. He took one last look at Verchiel and Camael locked in deadly combat, then spread his ebony wings wide to enfold them all.

"Nephilim!" Verchiel screamed as Aaron pictured Aerie in his mind. "You will not escape me!" And they were gone.

chapter eleven

Swords of fire came together with a deafening sound that reminded Camael of the birth cries of Creation. Slivers of heavenly flame leaped from the blades, burning shrapnel that eerily illuminated their twisted faces as he and Verchiel clashed.

Camael gazed sorrowfully at the scarred features of the creature before him, a once beatific being that had served the will of God, but had somewhere lost his way. He too bore scars, but his were deep inside, still-bleeding wounds of sacrifice for his chosen mission—for a path traveled alone. But this was not the time for philosophical musings, and Camael quickly returned his attention to the task at hand, the total annihilation of his foe.

"Surrender, Camael, and I shall see that you are treated fairly," Verchiel snarled over their locked blades. "It is the least I can do for one I once called friend."

Camael thrust his opponent away and propelled himself backward with the aid of his golden wings. *"Friend*, Verchiel?" he asked, landing in a crouch five feet away. "If this is how you treat your friends, I shudder to think of what you do to your enemies."

Thick black smoke from the burning bodies of Powers' soldiers billowed about the room, triggering the fire alarms and sprinkler systems.

"Humor?" Verchiel asked above the tolling bell as he took to the air with a powerful flap of his wings. "You *have* been amongst the monkeys too long," he observed coldly. "In matters of God and Heaven, there is no place for humor."

Camael propelled himself toward his adversary. "Aaron has often said that I lack a sense of humor," he said, pressing his attack. "I do so like to prove him wrong."

Verchiel parried a thrust from Camael's sword and carried through with a furious strike of his own, cutting a burning gash through Camael's shoulder.

"Listen to you," he said. "Proving yourself to the animals? You disgust me."

Driven by anger and pain, Camael attacked, a snarl of ferocity upon his lips, the swordplay driving Verchiel back through the rising smoke.

"Do you not remember what it was like?" Verchiel asked, his movements a blur as he blocked Camael's relentless rain of blows. "Side by side, meting out the word of God. Nothing could oppose us. We were Order incarnate, and Chaos bent to our every whim."

Camael leaned back as a swipe of Verchiel's sword narrowly missed his throat. "Until we became what we professed to fight." He stopped his attack, hoping that Verchiel would hear his words. "Bringers of destruction and fear. Chaos incarnate."

Verchiel's eyes widened in disbelief. "Are you so blinded by your insane beliefs that you cannot see what I'm trying to achieve?"

A whip took shape in his hand, and he lashed out with its tail of flame. The burning cord wrapped itself tightly around Camael's neck and instantly began to sear its way through his flesh. The pain was all-consuming as Camael felt himself pulled toward his enemy with a mighty yank.

"It was that accursed prophecy that brought pandemonium to the world," Verchiel said as he fought to pull Camael closer. "This belief in the Nephilim's redemptive powers has created bedlam; I only seek to stem the flow of madness."

The stench of his own burning sickened Camael. His wings frantically beat the air to maintain his distance from his adversary as he brought his sword up and severed the whip's embrace. "Why can you not face the reality of the prophecy?" he rasped. "The harder you try to stop it, the more it seems to fight to become true."

Camael dove backward, down into the densest smoke. He could no longer hear the clang of the fire alarm, but the water raining down from the sprinklers felt comforting upon his wounded throat. He touched down upon the wooden floor and willed himself to heal faster. There was so little time. The human authorities were certainly on their way; the battle would need to be brought promptly to a close, for Verchiel would think nothing of ending innocent lives in the pursuit of his goals.

Searching the wafting smoke above him for signs of his adversary, Camael thought of Aaron, of Aerie, of all he had saved from Verchiel's murderous throngs. *Has it been enough?* The unspeakable acts he had once perpetrated in the name of God as leader of the Powers filled him with self-loathing, and he wondered if he could ever forgive himself. *Will killing Verchiel and allowing the prophecy to be fulfilled finally be enough?* He stepped over bodies of angels burned black by his ferocity, continuing to scan the smoke-choked room for signs of movement.

"Have I told you my plan for this world, Camael?" asked Verchiel from somewhere nearby.

Camael tensed, sword ready. He tried to attune his senses to the environment, but the fire alarm and the fall of the sprinkler's artificial rain interfered with their acuity.

"I see a world of obedience." Verchiel's voice seemed to be shifting positions within the smoke. "A world where *my* word is law."

Camael's eyes scanned the billowing smoke. "Don't you mean God's word?"

The smoke to his right suddenly parted to reveal the formidable sight of his former second in command, a spear of orange fire in his grasp. "You heard me right the first time," Verchiel said, and let the weapon fly.

Camael reared back and brought his sword of fire to bear. He blocked the spear with the burning blade, but as it disintegrated in a flash of light, he felt another presence behind him. Still moving, he tossed his sword from right hand to left, spinning around to confront this new assailant.

Camael's blade struck armor the color of a blood-soaked battlefield and shattered. *Magick,* he thought, momentarily taken aback. He was about to formulate another weapon when he was struck from behind. A sword entered his body through his back; the white-hot blade exiting just below his ribcage in a geyser of steaming blood before being brutally pulled back.

Camael turned, a ferocious roar born of pain and rage escaping his lips. *How could I have been so reckless as to forget the hunter?* he thought, bringing his new sword of flame up to bite back at the coward who had struck from behind.

Verchiel blocked his swipe with the sword he had pulled from the angel's back.

"Do you know what I think, Camael?" Verchiel asked in a voice that dripped with madness.

Camael gasped as another blade, this one made of iron, was plunged into his back, and he felt himself grow suddenly weaker, the magicks infused within the knife sapping away his strength. He heard the armored warrior breathe heavily behind him, as if aroused by this craven act of savagery.

"I believe that the Creator has lost His mind," Verchiel said in a conspiratorial whisper. "Driven mad by the infectious disease of this virulent prophecy."

He stepped closer as Camael fell to his knees. The bleeding angel tried to stand, to carry on with the fight, but the metal blade had made that impossible.

"It has touched His mind in such a way that He actually believes what is happening here is right. How else can you explain it?" the demented angel asked. "God has become infected, as you were infected, and so many other pathetic beings that we so mercifully dispatched over the centuries."

Camael could taste his own blood and suspected that his time was at an end. He had always known that it would come to this; that his final battle would be against the one that had so twisted the will of God. "Will you attempt to mercifully dispatch the Creator as well?" he asked, disturbed by how weak his voice sounded.

The Powers' leader seemed horrified by this query. "You speak blasphemy," he proclaimed. "When my job is done, I will return to Heaven and see to the affairs of both Heaven and Earth until our Lord and Master is well enough to see to the ministrations of the universe on His own."

Camael could not hold back his laughter, although it wracked his body with painful spasms. "Do you hear yourself?" he asked through bloody coughs that flecked his bearded chin with gore. "You presume to know the grand schemes of He who created all things—He who created *us*." He averted his gaze, no longer able to look upon the foul creature before him. "If Lucifer could hear you now, he would embrace you as a like-minded brother," Camael added with a disgusted shake of his head.

"How dare you speak his name to me," Verchiel raged, falling down upon his own knees and grabbing Camael's face. "Everything I do, I do for the glory of His name. When this is done, and things have returned to the way they once were, I shall sit by His side, and all shall know that my actions were just."

Camael stared into Verchiel's dark eyes, falling into the depths of their insanity. "Things will never be as they were," he whispered, shaking Verchiel's hand from his face. "And they will call you monster."

Verchiel jumped to his feet, his scarred features twisted in fury. "Then monster I shall be," he shrieked as he raised his flaming sword and brought it down toward Camael's head.

Camael had been saving his strength, a small pocket of might that he hoped would enable him to return to Aerie. He reached behind himself, finding the knife that still protruded from his flesh. His hand closed around the hilt and he yanked the offending object from his back, bringing it around and up to meet the sword's deadly arc. Verchiel's weapon shattered on contact with the mystical metal, and the Powers' commander cried out, stumbling back as burning shrapnel showered his exposed flesh.

Camael unfurled his wings, thrusting them outward, hurling the scarlet-armored warrior away from him. His body screamed in protest, blood filling his mouth, but he did not let it deter him.

"You cannot hope to escape me, traitor!" Verchiel screamed, the mottled flesh of his face decorated with fresh burns. "You're already dead!"

Camael enfolded himself in the comforting embrace of his wings and willed himself away from the school, with Verchiel's furious words echoing through the recesses of his mind.

"Not quite yet," said the warrior on his way to the place hidden from him for so long, the place he now called home.

Verchiel stood in the gymnasium at Kenneth Curtis High School surrounded by the burning bodies of his soldiers. "We're close," he said to his fallen comrades, now nothing more than smoking heaps of ash.

Malak had retrieved his helmet and stood by his master's side, his face bruised and spattered with blood. The alarm bell continued to toll and the sprinklers rained down upon them. The wails of fire trucks could be heard from outside, and Malak howled softly in response to the sirens' cries. Verchiel turned to him and the warrior abruptly stopped.

"You've failed me," Verchiel told him, and the warrior cowered in the shadow of his disappointment.

"There is something in him, this Nephilim, that was not there in the others that I have hunted," Malak said in an attempt to explain his failure. He shook his head slowly, as if attempting to understand the perception himself. "A fire burns inside this one—a will to live." Malak looked up into the eyes of his master. "A purpose."

"Do you have it?" Verchiel asked, ignoring the ramblings of his servant. "Do you have the scent of our enemies?"

Malak nodded, a simpleton's grin of accom-

lishment spreading across his face. "They cannot hide from me anymore," he said, eyes twin-
ling mischievously. "Like blood in the white,
white snow; I can follow them."

"Excellent," Verchiel hissed. He would
remember this day, this very point in time when
his plan fell neatly into place.

Through the billowing smoke, he saw shapes
moving into the room, firefighters, their bodies
covered in heavy, protective layers of clothing.
In their hands they carried the tools of their
trade: high-powered flashlights, axes, and thick
hoses. Verchiel felt Malak bristle beside him.

"There's somebody in here," he heard one of
the firefighters say, his voice muffled by the oxy-
gen mask that covered his face.

A powerful flashlight illuminated the angel
and his servant. Verchiel did not hide himself,
instead he unfurled his wings and held his arms
out so they might gaze upon his magnificence.
Through the thick smoke and the clear masks
that covered their faces, he could see their eyes
bulge with fear and wonder, and reveled in their
awe of him.

Malak growled and from the air plucked a
fearsome sword, still encrusted with the blood of
a previous kill. He started toward the humans,
but Verchiel reached out, grabbing hold of his
armored shoulder.

"Leave them be," he proclaimed for all to
hear.

Two of the firemen had fallen to their knees
in supplication, while another fled in sheer
panic. Verchiel could hear their prayers.

"Let them look upon me and know that a
time is approaching when the sight of my kind
will be as common, and as welcome, as the
sunrise." Verchiel's voice boomed above the
sound of the fire alarm. "There are snakes living
amongst you," he proclaimed as he closed his
wings about himself and his servant. "And there
shall come a time of cleansing."

And as Verchiel willed himself away, he left
the firefighters with a final pronouncement.

"That time is now."

Aaron did as he was taught. He saw Aerie in his
head; the high, chain-link fence that ran around
its perimeter, the run-down homes, the weeds
pushing up through the cracks in the sidewalks.
In the beginning there was complete and utter
darkness, and then a sense of movement. It was
like traveling through a long, dark tunnel. He
opened his wings, pushing back the stygian
black that enveloped them and saw that they
had successfully arrived. He had rescued Vilma—
but at what price?

He looked around. They were standing in
front of Belphegor's home, and nearly every citi-
zen was waiting. The old fallen angel was sitting
in a beach chair at the sidewalk's edge, a sweat-
ing glass of iced tea in his hand. Lehash, looking

none too pleased, and Lorelei stood on either side of the multicolored chair. It was quiet in Aerie, quiet as the grave.

Aaron felt Vilma shiver in his arms and pulled her closer, gazing into her wide, dark eyes. "It's going to be all right," he whispered, holding her tighter.

"*Is she hurt?*" Gabriel asked, sniffing at her body.

Vilma writhed and her shirt rose up to reveal the angry burns on her belly.

"Oh, my God," Aaron said, starting to panic. "Somebody help me." He looked frantically at the people around him.

Lorelei moved forward and placed a hand on Vilma's brow.

"He hurt her . . . tried to trigger the change," Aaron said. "There are burns on her stomach and I . . . I think she's sick."

"I'll take her from here," Lorelei said, and gently began to pry the girl from his arms.

"Will she be okay?" He didn't want to let her go.

"She's been with Verchiel," Lorelei responded coldly as she removed her dungaree jacket, wrapping it around the shivering Vilma's shoulders. "I can only guess what that monster has done to her."

Lorelei began to lead Vilma away, and Aaron reached out to take hold of her arm. "Thank you."

She turned slowly to look at him; there was fear in her eyes. "Does that mean that you owe me?" Lorelei asked.

Aaron nodded as he let go of her arm. "Anything."

"Don't let them down," she whispered. "They've waited so long—sacrificed too much—to have it all taken away."

He had no idea how to respond, but Lorelei had already turned and was leading Vilma away. "C'mon, honey, let's see about getting you fixed up."

"Aaron?" Vilma suddenly protested.

He was going to her when Gabriel cut across his path. *"It's going to be just fine,"* the animal said to the girl, and the expression on her face told Aaron that she could understand the dog as well as he. Gabriel stretched his neck and nuzzled her hand lovingly. *"We'll go with Lorelei and she'll make you feel better, you'll see."* Gabriel looked back at Aaron. *"I'll go with her."*

Aaron nodded in approval and watched the threesome proceed down the street, Gabriel chatting reassuringly all the while. If only he could have the same level of confidence as his dog. He thought of Camael, who had yet to return, and icy fingers of dread took hold of his heart. He had to go back, back to Ken Curtis to help his friend. He turned to Belphegor. "I have to leave again; I have to help Camael."

He unfurled his wings, but pain shot through his body, driving him to his knees. His head throbbed and the stab wound in his shoulder was bleeding again, he could feel the snaking trail of warmth beneath his shirt.

"You need to rest," he heard Belphegor say evenly. "You're no good to anyone now."

"But he needs help!" Aaron said, fighting to get to his feet.

"Camael can take care of himself," Lehash barked. "He's fought many a battle without your help, Nephilim. You've done enough."

Aaron stared across the street at the gunslinger and Belphegor. Their faces were blank, insensate, as if they'd used up their lifetime allotment of emotion long ago. But it was in the faces of the others, the citizens, that he saw what he was responsible for. They milled about, eyes darting here and there, waiting for answers, waiting to have their fears put to rest. He could feel the anxiety coming off them in waves.

"I couldn't just leave her," he said to them. "I had to do something." He managed to get to his feet and lurched toward them, his angelic trappings fading as he drew closer. "I'm so sorry. It seemed right at the time, but now I . . ." He felt his strength wane and he suddenly sat down in the street, burying his face in his hands. "I just don't know what to think."

An aluminum chair leg scraped across the concrete sidewalk and he lifted his face to see that Belphegor was standing. The old fallen angel handed his nearly empty glass to Lehash, who stared at it with contempt. "Hold on to this," he told the constable, and moved toward Aaron.

It hurt to think. It felt as though Verchiel had touched his brain with a burning hand; his thoughts were a firestorm. There was so much he had to do—so much responsibility. Why did *he* have to be the Chosen One? he anguished. In his mind all he could see were the faces of those he had failed: his mom and dad, Dr. Jonas, Vilma . . . Stevie.

"They . . . he changed my little brother into a monster," Aaron said, gazing up into the elderly visage of Belphegor. "How could they do that to a kid?" he asked desperately as he ran a hand through his tangle of dark hair. "How could a creature of Heaven be so cruel?"

"Verchiel and his followers have not been creatures of Heaven for quite some time," Belphegor replied. "They lost sight of that special place a long time ago."

"Why can't he just leave me alone?" Aaron asked, the weight of his responsibilities beginning to wear upon him. "Why does it have to be this way?"

Belphegor sighed as he looked up at the early morning sky above Aerie. "Verchiel's still fighting the war, I think," he said after a bit of thought. "So caught up in righting a wrong, that he can't accept the idea that the battle is over. There's a new age dawning, Aaron." Belphegor slowly squatted down, and Aaron could hear the popping of his ancient joints. "Whether he likes it or not."

Aaron looked into the old angel's eyes, searching for a bit of strength he could borrow.

"And you're the harbinger," he continued. "Whether *you* like it or not."

"But I'm responsible for ruining this," Aaron said, motioning toward the neighborhood around them. "Verchiel and his Powers are probably coming here because of me."

"Looks that way," Belphegor said, calmly straightening up. "But we never expected it to be easy."

Lehash left the crowd of citizens and came to them. The constable's eyes had turned to dark, shiny marbles in the recesses of his shadowed brow. "Is this how he's going to save us?" he asked Belphegor, speaking loud enough for everyone to hear. "Crying in the street? I always expected that a savior would have more balls than that, but I guess I was wrong."

It couldn't have hurt worse if Lehash had pulled out his pistols and shot him again. The constable's words cut deep, and Aaron felt the power of angels surge through his body again. The sigils rose up on his flesh, his body afire as he leaped to his feet, his wings of shadow propelling him at the angel who had hurt him so.

"Do you want to see balls, Lehash?" he asked in a voice more animal than man. A sword of fire had materialized in his hand, and he stood ready to strike.

Lehash had drawn his golden guns. "Show me what you're gonna do when the Powers come for us, Nephilim," the gunslinger demanded, his thumbs playing with the hammers of his supernatural weapons. "Show me how powerful you are when they start to burn us alive."

Belphegor stepped between them, placing a hand on each of their chests. With little effort, he pushed them both apart. "This isn't going to help anything," the Founder of Aerie said, giving each a piece of his icy stare. "There's a storm coming, and no matter how much we rail against it—or one another—it doesn't change the fact that the rain is going to fall."

Aaron felt it at the nape of his neck, a slight tingle that made the hair stand at attention. He turned to see that something was taking shape in the air across the street from them.

"Camael?" Aaron asked, starting toward the disturbance.

Belphegor grabbed hold of his arm. "Wait," he demanded.

Aaron pulled away, certain that it was his

friend who had returned. Camael's wings spread wide to reveal him, and Aaron gasped at the sight. The angel clutched his stomach, blood flowing from a wound to stain the streets of Aerie. Camael pitched forward as Aaron ran to him.

"It comes," he heard Belphegor say in a foreboding whisper at his back. "The storm comes."

chapter twelve

𝕿here was so much blood.

Aaron cradled the body of the angel warrior in his arms, feeling Camael's life force ebbing away. He was reminded of that horrible day he had knelt in the middle of the street holding a dying Gabriel. He had never wanted to feel that way again, but here it was, as painful as the last time.

"I can do something," he said to his friend in an attempt to rally some confidence not only for Camael, but also for himself. Aaron reached deep within, searching for that spark of the divine that would allow him to save his mentor as he had his pet.

Camael took Aaron's hand in his. "Do not waste your strength on a lost cause, boy," he said, his grip firm, but weakening.

Aaron held the angel to him, gazing in mute

horror at the stab wounds in his friend's back. One was a blackened hole characteristic of a heavenly weapon's bite, but the other showed no sign of cauterization and bled profusely. "We'll stop the bleeding and you'll be all right," he told his friend, pressing his hand firmly against the wound.

Camael shuddered, and a fresh geyser of dark blood sprayed from the wound. The blood was warm, its smell pungent. "It will not stop." He struggled to sit up. "The enchanted metal and Verchiel's sword," he strained, "I fear it was a most lethal combination."

"Lie still, we can—"

Camael still held Aaron's hand and rallied his strength to squeeze it all the harder. "I did not return to have you save my pathetic life," the angel said, the intensity of his stare grabbing Aaron's attention and holding it firm. "I never considered that the prophecy would apply to me . . . that I could be forgiven."

"Stop talking like that," Aaron said, dismissing the fatalistic words of his mentor.

Many of the citizens who had gathered in front of Belphegor's home now stood in a tight circle around Aaron and Camael, watching the drama unfold. One of the men stripped off his T-shirt and offered it to Aaron to use as a compress against the angel's bleeding wound.

"I've saved many lives in my time on this world," Camael reflected. "But I don't believe it will ever balance the scales against the lives I took as leader of the Powers."

"How can you be sure, Camael?" Aaron asked in an attempt to keep his friend with him, to keep him focused. He gestured at the circle around them. "Most of them wouldn't be here. *I* wouldn't be here if it weren't for you."

Camael looked at him with eyes that had grown tired, eyes that had seen so much. "Deep down I knew that it was wrong, but still I kept on with the killing, for I believed that it was what *He* wanted of me. How sad that it took the writings of a human seer to force me to come to my senses." He laughed and dark blood spilled from his mouth to stain his silver goatee. "Imagine that," he said with a weary smile. "It took a lowly human to show me the error of my ways."

Aaron chuckled sadly. "Yeah, imagine that."

The angel warrior's body was suddenly wracked with spasms of coughing that threatened to shake away what little life there still was in his dying frame. Time, as it always seemed to be, was running out.

"Is he going to die?" one of the citizens, a girl probably only a few years older than Aaron, asked. There were tears in her eyes, and in the eyes of all present. He could not bring himself to answer, even though the inevitable seemed obvious.

"That is the burning question of the day,"

Camael answered, looking at Aaron. "Will I die here on the street of the place I sought so long to find?" He pulled Aaron closer as he asked the question, the source of the strength that had allowed him to return to Aerie. "Or might I actually be forgiven?" the angel asked wistfully. "Only you have the answer."

Aaron could sense that his friend's time was short. "Shall we find out?" he asked Camael, reaching down into the center of his being to find the gift of redemption. It was there, waiting for him as he imagined it would be. He called forth the heavenly essence, drawing upon it, feeling its might rise up and flow down his arm into one of his hands. The facility to redeem danced upon his fingertips, and Aaron looked compassionately to the angel that had shown him the road to his destiny. He wrestled with feelings of intense emotion: sadness, for he would not be seeing his friend again, and great happiness, for Camael would be going home.

Camael began to pray, his weary eyes tightly closed. "Have mercy upon me, O God. With the multitude of Your tender mercies, blot out my offenses."

Aaron brought his hand closer, the power contained within glowing like a small sun.

"Cleanse me from my sins. For I acknowledge my offenses, and they are ever before me."

His touch lighted upon Camael's chest and

Aaron felt the energy of his special gift swell and begin to flow from him. This was it. "You are forgiven," Aaron declared as his hand eerily slipped beneath the flesh of the angel's breast.

Camael gasped, his body arching as Aaron let go of the force collecting in his fingertips, releasing the power of redemption inside him. The angel's flesh began to fume. The skin grew brittle and fractured as the human shell that he had been wearing since his personal fall from grace began to flake away. Camael writhed upon the ground, like a snake sloughing off its skin, as the glory of what he once had been was revealed.

There came a jubilant cry of release, followed by a dazzling flash of brilliance, and Aaron instinctively turned away, the flash of the angel's rebirth blinding to the earthly eye. Aaron listened to the gasps and cries of awe from those that had gathered around them, and he turned his gaze back to the latest recipient of his heavenly gift.

Awesome, was all Aaron could think of as he watched the beautiful, fearsome creature floating on wings seemingly made from feathers of gossamer and sunlight. Camael's hair moved about his head like a halo of fire. His flesh was nearly translucent and he was adorned in armor that could easily have been forged from the rays of the sun. The angel noticed him then, and

Aaron finally understood the enormity of his responsibility. As he gazed at the magnificent entity before him, he knew it was his right and his alone. He *was* the One, and this was his burden and his joy.

"It must have been something," Aaron said to the transformed Camael, thinking of a time in Heaven before the strife . . . and wondering how it would be now when his friend returned.

"Maybe it will be something again," Camael said in a voice like the surge of ocean waves upon a beach, and turned his attention to the open sky above.

Aaron prepared himself for the being's ascension, but the angel seemed to hesitate, as if something was preventing him from moving on. "What's wrong, Camael?" he asked him.

"I . . . I do not wish to leave you with the burden of this responsibility," Camael said, longingly returning his gaze to the sky above him.

"I'll be fine," Aaron reassured him. "This is how it's supposed to be."

The two again exchanged looks, and Aaron could see that the angel was torn.

"Go, Camael," he said in a powerful voice that he hoped brimmed with authority. "Your job is done; it's time for you to go home."

With those words, Camael spread wide his wings and began his ascent to a world beyond this one. His wings of light and fire stirred the air, filling it with the gentle sounds of the wind. Aaron could not help but think that it sounded like the voices of small children singing.

"Say good-bye to Gabriel," the angel said. "I do believe I'll miss him."

"He has that effect," Aaron replied, and watched the glimmer of a smile cross the angel's blissful features.

Then Camael turned his full attention to the yawning space above him, raised his arms to the sky, and in a flash of light that seemed to warm Aaron to the depths of his soul, the angel that was his friend was gone.

Aaron stumbled back, the beauty of Camael's ascent still dancing before his eyes. He was on his own now, but he knew what needed to be done.

The Nephilim turned to face Belphegor and Lehash and was astonished to see that the citizens were kneeling on the street behind them, heads bowed in reverence. "What's all this?" he asked.

"They know the truth now," Belphegor said, a smile tugging at the corners of his mouth.

"Son of bitch," Lehash growled as he pulled the worn Stetson from his head. "You are the One."

Aaron walked toward Lorelei's house, wondering about Vilma's condition and how Gabriel would take the news of Camael's passing. At first meeting, the angel and the dog hadn't really gotten along, but recently, a strange, begrudging friendship seemed to have developed between the two.

He chanced a casual glance over his shoulder to see if he was still being followed, and sure enough, a sizeable number of Aerie's population trailed a respectful distance behind. Lehash, in the lead, politely tipped his hat. Aaron knew they were there because they believed he was something special—something many of them had been waiting for most of their lives—but the adoration made him uncomfortable. He wished they would admire him from their own homes.

He headed up the walk and climbed the few steps to the front door. As he pulled open the screen, he noted that the crowd had stopped at the street, watching him from a distance.

"I'll be right here if you need anything," the constable confirmed, taking up a guardian's stance at the beginning of the walk.

Aaron waved and stepped into the small hallway inside Lorelei's house. To the right was the living room. Vilma was lying on the overstuffed couch. She was asleep, her limp hand resting on Gabriel's side as he sat near her on the floor, resting his chin on the edge of the sofa. Lorelei sat at the edge of the rickety coffee table, applying tape to a bandage on Vilma's exposed stomach.

"Hey," Aaron said as he came into the room. "How's she doing?"

Gabriel lifted his head from the couch to look at Aaron. *"Hello,"* the dog said.

Lorelei finished her ministrations and gently pulled Vilma's shirt down to cover the dressing. "The burns were pretty bad," she said, packing up her supplies. "Looks like Verchiel had a good time with her," she added, jaw tightly clenched. "I've cleaned and dressed them using some special oils to help her heal faster. Physically, I'd say she's going to be fine."

"And mentally?" Aaron asked, struggling to contain his guilt. It was exactly what he had feared, one of the reasons he had left Lynn to begin with. Verchiel had used someone else to get at him.

Lorelei looked at the sleeping girl on the couch. "Remember, the whole process of becoming a Nephilim does quite the job on your head, and some of us are stronger than others."

Aaron nodded, knowing full well the painful truth of Lorelei's words.

"We'll just have to wait and see," she said, taking the leftover medical supplies back to the kitchen.

Aaron found himself staring at Vilma's face. He could see her eyes moving beneath her lids. *Dreaming,* he thought as he watched her, *and hopefully only the good kind.*

"Did Camael come back yet?" Gabriel asked as

he stood up and stretched, lowering his front body down to the ground while sticking his butt up into the air.

Aaron hesitated, not a good thing when dealing with a dog like Gabriel.

"He hasn't come back yet, Aaron?" the dog asked, showing concern as he completed his stretch. *"We should go look for him."*

Aaron squatted down, taking the yellow dog's head in his hands and rubbing behind his floppy ears.

"What's wrong?" the Labrador asked. *"I can sense that something isn't right."*

"Camael did come back, Gabe, and—"

"Then where is he?" the dog interrupted.

"Gabriel, please," Aaron said exasperated. "Let me finish."

Gabriel sat; his blocky head cocked quizzically to the side.

"Camael did come back," Aaron continued. "But he was hurt."

"Like I was hurt before you made me better?" the dog asked.

Aaron nodded, reaching down to stroke his friend's thick neck. "Yeah, like that, only I couldn't fix him."

Gabriel stared at his master, his chocolate brown eyes filled with a special intensity. *"What are we going to do?"*

He thought of how to explain this to the animal. Sometimes communicating with Gabriel was like talking to a little kid, and other times like an old soul with knowledge beyond his years. "Do you remember Zeke?" he asked, referring to the fallen angel who had first tried to tell him he was a Nephilim. Zeke had been mortally wounded during their first battle with Verchiel and his Powers.

"I liked Zeke," Gabriel said with a wag of his tail. *"But you did something to him and he went away. Where did Zeke go again, Aaron?"*

"I sent Zeke home," he explained. "I sent him back to Heaven."

"Just like the other Gabriel," his best friend said, refering to the archangel they had encountered in Maine a few weeks ago, whom Aaron had also released from his confines upon the Earth.

"Exactly," Aaron answered, petting the dog.

"Did you have to send Camael home, Aaron?" Gabriel asked, his guttural voice coming out as a cautious whisper.

Aaron nodded, continuing to scratch his four-legged friend behind his soft ears. "Yes, I did," Aaron said. "It was the only thing I could do for him." Of all the breeds of dogs that he had encountered while working at the veterinary clinic, it never ceased to amaze him how expressive the face of a Labrador retriever could be. He could tell that the dog was taking his news quite hard. "He told me to tell you good-bye—and that he'd miss you."

Gabriel slowly lowered himself to the floor, avoiding his master's watchful gaze. He placed his long face between his two front paws and sighed heavily.

Aaron reached out to stroke his head. "You okay, Gabe?" he asked tenderly, sharing the dog's sadness.

"I didn't get a chance to say good-bye to him," Gabriel said softly, his ears lowered in a mournful show of feelings.

Aaron lay down beside the big, yellow dog and put his arm around him. "I said good-bye for the both of us," he said, hugging the Lab tightly. And they lay there for a little while longer, both of them remembering a friend now gone from their lives.

The leader of the Powers host flew in the predawn sky, circling high above the Saint Athanasius Church and Orphanage. He could feel it in the atmosphere around him—change was imminent, and he reveled in it as the cool caress of the morning breeze soothed his healing flesh. *He* would be the harbinger of a new and glorious age.

Verchiel took his body earthward, gliding down toward the towering church steeple, where he clung to its side like some great predator of the air. He gazed down from his perch at the open space of the schoolyard below. *It is time,* he thought, time to call his army, to gather his troops for the impending war. Verchiel tilted back his head and let loose a wail that drifted on the winds, calling forth those that had sworn their allegiance to him and his holy mission. The cry moved through the air, beyond the confines of Saint Athanasius, to affect those still held tightly in the embrace of sleep.

A child of three awakened, screaming so long and hard that he ruptured a blood vessel in his throat, vomiting blood onto his Scooby Doo sheets. On the way to the emergency room, all he could tell his parents was that the bird men were coming and would kill everyone.

A middle-aged computer software specialist, recently separated from his wife, awoke from a disturbing dream, in his cold, one-bedroom apartment, determined that today would be the day he took his life.

A mother squirrel ensconced in her treetop nest of leaves, woke from a fitful rest and senselessly began to consume her young.

Verchiel ceased his ululating lament, watching with eager eyes as his army began to gather, their wings pounding the air. They circled above him like carrion birds waiting for the coming of death, then one by one began their descent. Some found purchase upon the weatherworn pieces of playground equipment, others roosted on the eaves of the administration building, and the remainder stood uncomfortably on the ground, hands clasped behind their backs.

Verchiel was both saddened and enraged by how their numbers had dwindled; victims of the Nephilim and those that believed in the validity of the prophecy. *They will not have died in vain*, he swore, spreading his wings, dropping from the steeple to land on the rusted swingset, scattering his warriors in a flurry of beating wings. All eyes were upon him as he raised himself to his full height, balanced on the horizontal metal pole. Today victory would belong to him. He raised his arm, and in his outstretched hand formed a magnificent sword of fire, the Bringer of Sorrow.

"Look upon this sword," the leader of the Powers proclaimed, "for it shall be your beacon." He felt their adoration, their belief in him and his mission. "Its mighty light will shine before us, illuminating the darkness to rout out evil. And it will be smited," he roared, holding out the sword to each of them.

Their own weapons of war took shape in the hands of those gathered before him, and they returned the gesture, reestablishing a camaraderie that was first forged during the Great War in Heaven. A buzz like the crackle of an electrical current moved through the gathering, and he saw that Malak had arrived, bloodred armor polished and glistening in the light. *What a spectacular sight*, Verchiel thought. No finer weapon had he ever created.

Malak walked among the angels, an air of confidence surrounding him like a fog. Their eyes were upon him, filled with a mixture of awe and disdain. Some of the angels did not approve of the power that had been bestowed upon the human animal, but they dared not speak their disfavor to Verchiel. They did not understand human emotions, and were not able to see the psychological advantage he now held over his accursed enemy. But when Malak rendered helpless the one called Aaron Corbet, and the Nephilim's life was brought to an end, they would have no choice but to concede to the hunter's superiority.

"The smell of our enemy calls out to me," Malak declared, his voice cruel, echoing through the cold metal of his helmet.

"Then let us answer that call," Verchiel ordered from his roost.

With those words Malak spun around, an imposing sword of black metal in his grasp. As if delivering a deathblow to an opponent, he sliced through the air, creating a doorway to another place, the place where their final battle would be fought.

"Onward," the Powers' leader exclaimed. "It is the beginning of the end."

The angels of the Powers' host cried out as one, their mighty wings taking them aloft, through the tear in reality.

And as Verchiel watched them depart, he

remembered something he had once read in the monkeys' holy book, written by one called Isaiah, he believed. *"They shall have no pity on the fruit of the womb; their eye shall not spare children.*

Verchiel smiled. He couldn't have voiced it better himself.

chapter thirteen

Gabriel was feeling sad.

No matter how hard he tried, with pleasant thoughts of delicious things to eat, chasing after balls, and long naps in warm patches of sunshine, the dog could not shake the unhappy state of mind. How he wished the human idea that animals didn't experience emotion was not just a myth.

As he trotted beside Aaron down the center of an Aerie street, Gabriel thought of the long and difficult night they had just passed. Neither had slept much as they watched over Vilma and shared the pain of Camael's passing. The dog gazed up at his friend, studying the young man's face in the early morning light. His expression was intense, determined, but Gabriel could sense the pain that hovered just beneath the surface.

Their lives had suddenly become so hard. Gabriel thought longingly of days—*Could it have only been just weeks ago?*—spent going for long walks, licking cookie crumbs from Stevie's face, cuddling with the Stanleys as they rubbed his belly.

The sound of a door slamming roused the Lab from his reflection, and he turned his blocky head to see another of Aerie's citizens leaving his home to join the crowd already on their way to the gathering.

Gabriel felt his hackles begin to rise. Verchiel was coming and he would probably be bringing Stevie along with him. He was no longer the little boy Gabriel so fondly remembered, but something that filled him with fear. Images of his battle with the armored monster at the school gym flooded his thoughts. It hadn't taken more than a moment for him to realize who he was facing; the scent of the boy—of Stevie—was there in the form of the one called Malak, but the smell was wrong. It had been changed, made foul. Last night Gabriel had struggled with a way in which to express to his master what his senses perceived, but Aaron already knew that Stevie had become Malak. Although Gabriel couldn't understand exactly what had happened to Stevie, he shared Aaron's deep shock at the little boy's transformation.

A sudden, nagging question formed in the

Lab's mind and he stopped walking, waiting for Aaron to notice that he was no longer at his side. Finally Aaron turned.

"What's up?" the boy asked him.

Gabriel shook his head sadly, his golden brown ears flopping around his long face. *"Stevie's been poisoned. It's like this place,"* he said. *"It was nice before, but something bad has happened to it. Do you understand what I'm trying to say?"*

Aaron walked back and laid a gentle hand on the dog's head. "I get it," he said.

Citizens passed on their way to the meeting place, but the two friends paid them no mind.

Gabriel licked Aaron's hand, then looked nervously into his eyes. *"It's Stevie, but it's not. His smell is all wrong."*

Aaron nodded quickly. "I understand," he said, a troubled expression on his face as he turned to join the others heading toward the church at the end of the street. "C'mon, we better get going."

Gabriel followed at his side, struggling with the dark question he did not want to ask. But it was one he knew that Aaron had to confront. *"What will you do if he tries to kill you again, Aaron?"* Gabriel asked gently.

Aaron did not answer, choosing to remain silent, but the expression upon his master's face told Gabriel everything he needed to know, and it just made the dog all the sadder.

† † †

Lehash stood nervously in Aerie's old church, where he had never stood before, attempting to communicate with a higher being he had not wanted to speak with for many a millennium.

He studied the crude picture of the savior painted on the altar wall. The child did not look like Aaron Corbet, with its bald head and bulging white eyes, but there was no doubt in the angel's mind of the boy's true identity. He had witnessed Aaron's power with his own eyes, and had been forever changed by it.

Lehash turned the Stetson nervously in his hands. "I . . . I don't know what to say," he stammered, his voice like sandpaper rubbing on wood. "I never imagined the day that I would speak to You again—never mind *want* to speak to You."

The fallen angel didn't care for what he heard in his voice: It sounded weak, scared, but at the moment, that was exactly what he was. "I never imagined You to have so much mercy," he said to the silence of the church. "To pardon what we did."

Lehash chuckled, looking about the room, then at the hat in his hands. "I used to feel sorry for the others—that they actually believed that You were going to forgive us. So many times I wanted to grab them by the shoulders and give 'em a good shake. *Don't you remember what we did?* I wanted to scream at them. But I kept my mouth shut."

Lehash slowly dropped to his knees and focused his gaze on the painting above the altar. "But I was wrong," he said, his voice filled with a sudden strength. "All these years here and I still don't know anything more than when I decided to join up with the Morningstar."

The fallen angel bowed his head and summoned forth wings that had not unfurled since his fall from Heaven. It was painful at first and he gritted his teeth as the atrophied appendages gradually emerged.

"What I'm trying to say is that I'm sorry for what I did in the past and what I'm going to do—and if I should die in battle today, I hope You can find it in Your heart to forgive me."

He had summoned forth his guns of gold and crossed them over his chest, spreading his wings as wide as he could. "But if not, I understand, 'cause for what I intend to do to Verchiel and his lapdogs, I wouldn't let me back into Heaven either."

The church door opened behind him and he quickly stood, wishing away the wings that had not touched the sky since his descent. "I said I didn't want to be disturbed," he barked, before realizing that it was Belphegor striding down the center aisle toward him. "Oh, sorry," Lehash said quickly as he reached for his hat that had dropped to the floor.

"Quite all right," Belphegor said, looking at

the altar painting. "Did you find what you were looking for?"

The constable thought for a moment. He had no idea if the Creator had been listening, but for the first time in longer than he could remember, he felt a certain sense of hope. "Y'know, I think I might have," he finally answered as he slipped the black Stetson down upon his head.

"That's good," Belphegor replied, and said no more.

And the two of them walked together toward the exit, and the gathering that awaited them beyond it.

Lorelei studied her reflection in the cracked, full-length mirror hanging on the back of her closet door. The vertical break in the reflective surface split the image of her, the two sides slightly out of sync with each other. She'd always thought about replacing it, but never seemed to have the time. She found the duality of the reflection depicted there strangely accurate, for since the emergence of her other half, the Nephilim side, struggle had been a constant in her life.

Lorelei ran a brush through her long, snow-white hair and wondered why she was bothering. *Have to look good for the slaughter, I guess,* she thought sardonically. Since arriving in Aerie she had known this day would come, the day that the Powers would try to kill them all. She shuddered, racked by a sudden chill of unease. She had seen what Verchiel and his kind were capable of, and the thought of facing them in battle filled her with dread.

She tossed her brush onto the bed and looked upon her trembling hands. Lorelei was afraid of what was to come. Part of her—some primitive, selfish part—wanted to run, to hide, but that side cared nothing for the future, for destiny. All that it concerned itself with was its continued survival. Taking some deep breaths, she attempted to calm the scared, animal side— the human nature—a single thought running through her head. *I am Nephilim and I have a destiny to fulfill.*

Lorelei grabbed her jacket from the bed and slipped it on, flipping out the snow-white hair from beneath her collar. "So what do you think?" she asked her cracked reflection as she adjusted the coat's fit. "Do you think he's really the One?" She had no idea, and doubted that the image looking back at her was any more knowledgeable. What she did know was that Aaron was something very special, and that was exactly what Aerie needed to survive this day. She only hoped that she would be strong enough to help him.

Leaving her bedroom, on the way to the gathering, she stopped in the living room to check on her patient. Lorelei sat on the couch next to the still-sleeping Vilma, and carefully checked beneath the bandage on her stomach. She was pleased; Verchiel had hurt the girl badly, but it looked like she was going to be all right, although she still had to survive the process of becoming a Nephilim.

Gently Lorelei placed her hand against the girl's perspiring brow, and Vilma's large, dark eyes suddenly opened. Her gaze darted about the room, then focused on Lorelei.

"I'm safe?" she asked groggily.

"Yes, you are," Lorelei answered in a soothing voice. "No one will hurt you anymore." She hoped that she was telling the truth, remembering the battle still to come.

A smile spread across the young woman's face. "He saved me," she said, obviously talking of Aaron, and Lorelei took strength from the moment.

"I think he's going to save us all," she told Vilma, suddenly confident that they would live to see tomorrow.

Aaron and Gabriel approached the crowd gathered before the Church of Aerie.

"It looks like everyone is here," Gabriel said as he looked around at the waiting crowd.

There was a nervous tension in the air as fallen angels and Nephilim stood side by side, the first generation of heavenly beings rubbing elbows with the next. For the first time Aaron truly understood what Aerie was all about. It was about change, for the Nephilim would be what remained upon Earth after the fallen angels were finally forgiven and allowed to return to Heaven. *A changing of the guard*, Aaron thought.

The crowd started to notice his arrival and stepped back, bowing their heads in respect, opening a path for him to the steps of the church.

"That's very nice of them," Gabriel commented as they walked past the citizens.

Some of those gathered gingerly reached out and touched his arms, his shoulders and back, barely audible words of thanks leaving their mouths. He wanted to tell them to stop. He wanted to tell them that he had done nothing that they should be thanking him for—in fact, they should be chewing his head off for drawing Verchiel's attention to Aerie's location.

A murmur passed through the crowd, and Aaron saw that Belphegor and Lehash had come out of the building and now waited for him at the top of the church steps.

This is it, he thought, starting his ascent.

"I'll wait for you down here," Gabriel said with a wag of his tail.

As he reached the top of the stairs, the two fallen angels bowed their heads as well. "Don't do that," he told them uncomfortably.

"Just showin' the proper respect," Lehash

said as he clasped his hands in front of himself.

Belphegor placed a firm hand upon his shoulder and looked into Aaron's eyes. "They know what is coming," he said, nodding toward the crowd gathered below them. "But they need to hear it from you—they need to know your intentions."

Aaron could feel their eyes upon him, the intensity of their gazes boring into his back. "Wouldn't it be better if you talked to them?" he suggested. "They trust you."

"Don't sell yourself short, boy," Lehash told him. "They know the real thing when they see it. It's you they've been waitin' for."

Aaron looked back to Belphegor, hoping the old angel would help him out. He'd never been comfortable with public speaking.

"The citizens are waiting" was all Belphegor said as he stepped back.

And Aaron knew there was only one thing left for him to do. Slowly he turned to face the throng and his breath was taken away by the sight of them; every eye fixed upon him, every ear attuned, waiting for what he was about to say. His mind went blank and all he could do was to return their stare. *Who am I kidding?* he asked himself, sheer panic setting in. They were insane to be depending on him. He wasn't a savior; he couldn't even help his family or his friends.

He looked into the crowd and saw Gabriel

staring up at him from the throng, the gaze of his dark brown eyes touching Aaron's, helping to bring a sense of calm to him. Farther back he noticed a distinct head of beautiful, white hair, and Lorelei giving him the thumbs-up.

"I don't want to disappoint you," Aaron said, his voice tenuous as the words began to spill from his mouth. "Some of you believe that I'm a savior, someone who's come to save the day." Aaron paused, looking out over the citizens of Aerie. "Am I the Chosen One?" he asked, feeling strength come into his words as he spoke from his heart. "I don't really know. But I do know that I have a power—a power that seems to set me apart from everyone else. And we'll never get to know what I am and what I'm capable of, if Verchiel has anything to say about it."

A rumbling murmur went up from the crowd and Aaron could only imagine the fear that many of them had lived with during their lives, dreading the day when the leader of the Powers host would turn his attention to them, and the place of peace that they had built for themselves.

"This morning I'm asking you to fight," Aaron told them. "To fight for your future—for your redemption, and your right to go home." He tried to look each in the eye. "This is what I intend to do," he told them. "It's time that I confronted my destiny—and I would be honored to have you all fight by my side."

The silence was deafening. Aaron wasn't exactly sure what he had expected, but a void of response was not necessarily what he'd hoped for. He was about to turn to Belphegor, when a sword of fire sprang to life within the crowd. It was raised high in the air, and was followed by another, and then another still. Aaron was speechless, looking out over the crowd, as every one of them raised a weapon of heavenly fire in salute to him.

"Guess that's a vote of confidence," Aaron heard Lehash say. He turned to find the constable wielding his golden pistols. "They're not swords, but they do pack a pretty good wallop," he said, crossing the weapons in front of his chest. "And I would be honored to fight in your name."

Belphegor smiled as Aaron looked back to the citizens.

Maybe we do have a chance, he thought, his faith roused by the sight of those gathered below him, and he wondered if Camael would have been proud. His musings on his absent friend were cut off, as there came a sound, abrupt in its intensity, painful to the ears. It was like the crack of an enormous bullwhip, and it was followed by a terrible ripping as a hole opened in the air above the crowd. Aaron watched with increasing horror as a red-garbed warrior dropped from the wound in space to the ground below. The crowd pulled back as Malak raised his spear, pointing it toward the Nephilim. Above the armored warrior, the gash pulsed and sparked as the sound of flapping wings began to fill the air.

This is it, Aaron thought as Lehash pushed past him down the stairs, pistols of heavenly fire in each hand. Gabriel had come up the stairs to Aaron's side, barking and baring his teeth in a display of savagery uncommon to the normally docile animal.

"I want you to go to Vilma," Aaron told him.

"But I want to stay with—"

"Don't argue, Gabriel," he ordered the dog. The sounds of angels' wings grew louder. "Protect Vilma." He knew that his friend would have preferred to stay at his side, but Vilma needed a guardian, and he could think of no one that he trusted more.

With no further argument, the dog bounded down the stairs and up the street.

And then an army of angels, bloodthirsty screams upon their lips, weapons of war in their hands, spewed forth from the hole, like biblical locusts preparing to blight the land.

chapter fourteen

Aaron had begrudgingly accepted his inhumanity, and now attempted to wear it with pride. There was very little pain as the sigils appeared on his flesh and his powerful wings burst from his shoulder blades. A spectacular sword of fire ignited in his hand, and he welcomed the rush of power that engorged every fiber of his being.

The last of the Powers' soldiers emerged from the tear in the fabric of space, and they began their assault, dropping down from the sky, their weapons of flame seeking to end the lives of Aerie's citizens. He wanted to help them, but he could not take his eyes from Malak—his little brother—still standing before the fissure.

What are you waiting for? Aaron wondered. The report of Lehash's pistols echoed like thunder through the normally still air, and then

Malak knelt on one knee, bowing his helmeted head before the opening. Aaron tried to see into the rip, certain that the surprises from the other side were not yet over.

A sudden chill filled the air, and Aaron felt his presence before seeing him. Verchiel emerged into Aerie as if he were its savior, and not it's destroyer. Wings of the purest white spread full, he glided from the darkness of the fissure, a look of contentment on his pale, aquiline features.

Just seeing the leader of the Powers there in the citizens' place of solace filled Aaron with a barely controlled fury. It was all he could do not to launch himself at the villain, but caution was the victor, and he waited for his enemy to make the first move.

"And so it ends," the Powers' leader proclaimed, his voice booming over the cries of battle. Verchiel glanced at his soldiers in the midst of violence, at the citizens fighting for their lives, and then his dark, hawklike eyes fell upon Aaron. "You couldn't possibly have believed it would end any other way!" Verchiel roared, smiling with anticipation.

Aaron leaped from the church's steps and landed on the sidewalk, sword of fire at the ready. "It's not over yet," he said to the angel beckoning to him with an outstretched hand.

Verchiel shook his head with great amusement. "No, Nephilim," he said, touching his long, spidery fingertips to the top of the kneeling Malak's helmet. "Another wants the honor of ending your life."

Malak slowly stood to face Aaron; a lance of black metal clutched in his armored hands.

"I believe he wants to eat your heart," the angel said, lovingly brushing imaginary dust from the shoulder of the warrior's scarlet armor. "And I do not wish to deny my pet his desire." Verchiel brought his hand to his mouth, kissed his fingertips, and placed them on Malak's head. "Kill him," the angel declared.

And with his master's blessing, Malak attacked.

Lehash had known the angels that now attacked him and the citizens of Aerie. Once they had been soldiers of Heaven, protecting the sanctity of the Creator's desires, but now they were something altogether different. These were not beings of purity and righteousness, but shadows of their former glory, twisted by the malignant beliefs of their leader.

He fired his weapon into the screaming face of one attacker, spinning around to kill another before the first could fall to the ground. It had been quite some time since he'd delivered violence on such a level, and he found that he had developed a distaste for it. Aerie had been good for him, calming what seemed to be an eternally angry spirit. He had found a place to belong, a home to replace the one that was lost to him.

But now there was a chance, a slim possibility, that he might see Heaven again, and somebody wanted to take that from him—from all of them who called Aerie their home. Lehash was not about to surrender that chance no matter how small. That was what fueled him.

He shot his bullets of fire, hoping that each enemy falling dead from the sky would bring him closer to forgiveness—closer to Heaven. But there were so many, and the air was soon filled with the stink of burning flesh and spilled blood.

What a terrible thing, the fallen angel thought as he unleashed the full fury of his terrible weapons, and watched as both friends and foes died around him.

What a terrible price to pay for forgiveness.

"Do you remember me, Stevie?" Aaron asked the creature before him. "Do you remember who I am?"

Malak thrust his spear forward with blinding speed, and Aaron reacted barely in time to angle his body away from its razor-sharp metal tip.

"I remember," Malak said, his voice cold and menacing as it echoed from inside the horned helmet. "I remember the pain you caused, the misery you have brought to the world."

He spun around gracefully, the spearhead slashing across the front of Aaron's body with an ominous whisper. The Nephilim moved too slowly and the tip of the spear passed through his shirt to cut a fine line from his left shoulder down to the right side of his stomach. He leaped back, feeling warm blood seeping from the open wound. First blood was to Malak, and Aaron doubted it would be the last of it spilled in this battle.

"I'm your brother," he tried again, preparing himself for the next assault. "Verchiel killed our parents. He took you, changed you, turned you into something—"

Like a rampaging bull Malak charged, the spear suddenly gone, replaced by a fearsome club, its surface studded with spikes. "He made me a hunter," he growled. "A killer of Heaven's criminals."

Aaron dove beneath the club's pass, discarding his own sword of fire and lunging forward to grab his attacker's weapon. They struggled for control of the instrument of death, but then Malak slammed his armored face into the bridge of Aaron's nose. Aaron heard a wet snap and blood exploded from his nostrils. It felt as though his head was about shatter, but he maintained his grip on the club.

Malak violently wrenched the weapon away, watching as Aaron stumbled backward, wiping the blood from his face. There was no pause in the creature's reaction, not the slightest hint of mercy. The armored warrior came at him again, and Aaron called upon a sword of fire to defend himself. The club had become a two-handed ax, and it descended on him with incredible force. He brought his own blade up and the collision of heavenly fire with enchanted metal rang in Aaron's ears like the crack of doom.

Both combatants leaped back, a brief respite before continuing their skirmish. Aaron became aware of the battles going on around him. The streets of Aerie echoed with the sounds of strife, and he wondered if it would have been the same if he had listened to Belphegor and not gone to Vilma's aid.

Feelings of guilt fueling him, Aaron took the offensive, charging at Malak, the tip of his fiery sword tracing a sparking line across the enchanted chest armor. Malak stepped back, discarding his ax and reaching for another instrument of death from his seemingly endless magickal arsenal. Aaron did not wait to see what the warrior would choose. With the aid of his flapping wings, he propelled himself forward and relentlessly rained blows upon his enemy with his own sword of fire.

"I don't know what he's told you!" Aaron shouted, desperate to reach some trace of his brother, even as he drove Malak back. "But it isn't true."

"You are a master of deceit," Malak said, drawing his own sword of dark metal to parry Aaron's blows. The warrior moved with inhuman speed, his movements registering as little more than a scarlet blur. "Lies flow from your mouth like blood from a mortal wound."

"Listen to me, Stevie!" Aaron yelled, on the defensive again, barely stopping the unremitting fall of the enchanted black blade.

"*Malak*," his attacker bellowed, enraged. "I am Malak!" The savagery of his attack intensified. "I kill you now in *his* name," Malak growled, preparing to deliver a final deadly strike.

And as Aaron primed himself to counter this killing blow, the question of futility echoed through his frenzied thoughts. *Is it possible?* He caught sight of the warrior's eyes through the slits of the horned helmet—murderer's eyes, void of any trace of humanity—and wondered if there was even a slight chance that Stevie was still somewhere inside the monster that was Malak.

Verchiel grinned, pleased by the ferocity of his pet's attack. Everything was proceeding as planned. He looked out over the dilapidated human neighborhood, at the battles being fought in his name. The vermin would be routed from their place of concealment, and the process of purging the last believers of the prophecy from the world of God could begin. After Aerie was wiped from existence, it would only be a matter of time before all the Creator's offenders were destroyed. And on that day he would return to Heaven, to the accolades of the Almighty, and he would take his place at God's side.

The Powers' leader breathed in the stench of violence, his memories taking him back to a time when his purpose was defined for him. He remembered the war in Heaven and how even when it appeared to be over, the followers of the Morningstar defeated, the true struggle had yet to begin. They took their audacity, their insolence, and fled to the Earth, hoping to escape the Creator's wrath. *To think that they actually believed they would be forgiven,* the angel mused.

"Lost in thought, Verchiel?" A voice distracted him from his reflection.

Verchiel looked toward the entrance of the church and gazed upon the living dead. "Belphegor," the Powers' commander hissed. "Camael told us that he had taken your life in the Garden."

"I think he may have exaggerated the truth a bit," the Founder of Aerie commented.

His disappointment in Camael strengthened all the more, Verchiel started up the church steps two at a time. "What is it the humans say?" he muttered, murder on his mind. "If you want a job done right . . ."

Belphegor did not respond. Instead he opened the door of the church and slipped inside.

Verchiel suspected a trap, but the idea that one he believed destroyed so long ago was still among the living drove him forth. He summoned his weapon of choice, and the Bringer of Sorrow came to burning life in his hand as he took hold of the cold metal of the handle and yanked the door wide, plunging himself into the place of worship with the hunger of bloodlust beating in his chest. The church was enshrouded in darkness, the only light from candles burning before a makeshift altar in the front of the building. Belphegor waited for him there.

"Come in, come in," the old angel said as he motioned Verchiel closer. "I was hoping to have a discussion with you before things got out of hand." He shrugged. "I guess we're a little late."

Verchiel began moving cautiously down the center aisle; the flames of his sword illuminating the church's interior with its wavering light. "I have nothing to discuss with the likes of you," he snarled as he surveyed the offensive surroundings.

Belphegor smiled as if privy to some secret knowledge. "That is where you're wrong, Verchiel," he corrected. "There is much to talk about." He turned to the mural painted upon the wall. "Have you seen this?" the fallen angel asked, gesturing to the depiction of an unholy trinity.

Verchiel sneered. "I have borne witness to

myriad representations of this repugnant prediction in my pursuits. I cannot begin to tell you how it disgusts me."

Belphegor nodded. "I figured that would be your answer."

"It is heresy to even think that the Lord God would allow—"

"He has, Verchiel," Belphegor interrupted. "He *has* allowed it. The prophecy has come true—you've seen it with your own eyes, but you're too damn stubborn to accept it."

The leader of the Powers seethed, the fallen angel's barbed words stoking the fires of his wrath. "The Creator has entrusted me with a mission that I intend to fulfill; those who sinned against Him will be held accountable for their crimes."

Belphegor moved toward him, defiance in his ancient eyes. "And what of our greatest sinner?" the fallen asked. "How is it that the first of the fallen was allowed to sire the savior of us all? Doesn't that tell you something, Verchiel? Doesn't that convince you that there might be some truth in the ancient writings?"

Sounds of the violence outside drifted into the place of worship, but it was nothing compared to the deafening din inside the angel's head. "The first of the fallen sired nothing," Verchiel roared, startled by his own fury. "We saw to that. Any woman who lay with him was destroyed. There was no chance of his seed taking root—"

"Not only did the seed root, but it bore fruit," Belphegor said, his voice firm with certainty.

Verchiel steeled himself, gripping his weapon all the tighter. "It cannot be," he whispered incredulously.

Belphegor shrugged again. "Mysterious ways and all that." He smiled and turned his gaze back to the mural. "Don't you see, Verchiel, it must be what *He* wanted—and if the Morningstar can be forgiven, there's hope for us all."

The church walls seemed to be closing in upon Verchiel, the revelation of the Nephilim's sire testing his limits. Did he have the might to hold on to his sacred mission? He felt it begin to slip from his grasp. *How could this have happened?* The question reverberated in his skull.

"Is it so outrageous to believe that we can be forgiven?" Belphegor asked him, the question like a dagger strike to his chest.

"Lies!" Verchiel shrieked, his wings unfurling as he strode down the remainder of the aisle toward the altar.

He pointed his blade toward the mural and the fire from his weapon streamed forth to scorch the painted image black. And then Belphegor's hands were suddenly upon his shoulders, and he was hurled backward into the rough benches, reducing them to kindling.

"You must face the truth!" Belphegor shouted, the altar burning behind him. "You are going against *His* wishes!"

Verchiel rose from the small pile of rubble, the power of his righteous fury building inside him. He remained silent, knowing what he must do.

"But it's not too late . . . ," Belphegor continued.

Verchiel's body began to glow, his clothing burning away to reveal flesh like cold, white marble. The floor beneath him began to smolder and the wood ignited.

"You, too, could be forgiven for your sins."

The Powers' commander spread open his wings and the fire of his heavenly being emanated from his body in waves.

"We could all go home, Verchiel," Belphegor pleaded, as his own flesh began to blister.

Then Belphegor burned.

As would they all.

Malak wielded two daggers, slashing and darting forward with the murderous grace of a venomous serpent. He seemed tireless in his pursuit of Aaron's demise, and the Nephilim found his defenses beginning to wane.

He didn't want to remember his little brother as the monster attacking him now, so he kept the memories of the child he loved at the forefront of his thoughts, drawing strength from emotion. With both hands he brandished a large broadsword of pulsing orange flame, swinging it around as opportunity presented itself. The flat of the blade connected with Malak's wrist, knocking one of the knives from his grasp in a flash of sparks as heavenly fire met magickally fortified armor.

Aaron heard a hiss of pain and anger from beneath the crimson face mask as Malak clutched his wrist to his chest. Although the blade could not penetrate the armor, the fragile flesh beneath would certainly suffer with the powerful force of the blow.

"It doesn't have to be like this, Stevie," Aaron said desperately. He just couldn't bring himself to give up.

But Aaron's futile attempts only served to enflame Malak's anger all the more, and the armored warrior came at him yet again. As he ducked and wove beneath the assassin's blows, Aaron knew a part of him was holding back. He also knew that if he didn't wise up fast, that part would get him killed. Malak was *not* Stevie. He had to accept that before he could bring this battle to a close.

Aaron sailed up into the air as Malak swiped at him with a short-bladed sword. He reached down and grabbed the armored warrior beneath the arms, ebony wings pounding the air to hold them aloft. Malak struggled in his clutches as the Nephilim strained to carry him higher and higher still. When the Powers' assassin violently threw back his head, jabbing one of the horns on his helmet into the tender flesh of

Aaron's stomach, the young man lost his grip, letting Malak plummet to the street below. Aaron watched the scarlet figure fall, fighting the urge to swoop down and save him. Malak hit the ground with a sickening clatter, his limp form tumbling to a stop in the center of the street.

The Nephilim swooped down from above to land beside the motionless body. Feeling the pangs of guilt, wishing he could hate the armored warrior, he reached out with both hands to pull the fearsome metal mask from the assassin's head. Aaron wanted to see the killer's face again, to look into his eyes, to find his little brother still alive somewhere within. He pulled off the horned helmet and discarded it, carefully placing a hand behind his neck and lifting his head. A single stream of red trickled from Malak's left nostril.

Malak's eyes slowly opened and Aaron tensed. The man's body shuddered and then coughed. "Aaron?" he said in a voice that sounded as if it came from a hundred miles away.

It was weak, but there was something in it that Aaron recognized. He pulled the young man closer, daring to believe there could be a chance, no matter how small. "I'm here," he told him, enfolding them both in the great expanse of his wings.

"Aaron . . . ," Malak said again, his voice strained and full of pain.

"Hold on now, we'll fix you," Aaron reassured him, certain now that Stevie was still in there somewhere, fighting for his identity, fighting against the pain and misery that Verchiel had used to distort him. He could see the struggle behind the man's deep blue eyes and Aaron held him tighter, lending him his strength. "Belphegor and Lorelei—they'll have the answers. We'll make it right, you'll see. Hang on, Stevie," he urged.

Slowly Stevie reached up to touch his brother's face, his gauntleted fingers tracing the black sigils.

"We'll be a family again, me and you . . . and Gabriel." Aaron laughed desperately, overcome with emotion. "Can't forget him."

He saw it in the man's eyes before he had a chance to react. Stevie had lost his battle. Malak closed his hand around Aaron's throat and started to squeeze. The grip was remarkable, cutting off his air supply completely as the metal-clad fingers dug into the tender flesh of his throat.

"Aaron," Malak said again, only this time it was more like a reptilian hiss, absent of any emotion.

The Nephilim grabbed Malak's wrist with both hands, struggling to break his grip. But Malak held fast, giggling maniacally. Explosions of color blossomed before his eyes and Aaron knew that it wouldn't be long before he blacked out. He spread his wings and began to beat the air, stirring up a storm of dirt and rock as he fought to be free, but it did nothing to loosen the hunter's grip upon his neck. Malak seemed to be enjoying the struggle, as if he too knew it was only a matter of time now.

Aaron's wings faltered and a trembling weakness spread through his arms. He gazed into the cold, dead eyes of the thing that used to be his brother and opened his mouth to scream. It was nothing more than a croak, but to the Nephilim's ears, it was a cry of mourning, a cry of rage for what had been done to an innocent little boy.

Malak smiled as Aaron let one of his hands fall away from the monster's wrist.

But the Nephilim wasn't giving up yet. From the arsenal inside his head, he selected a knife, a sleek and deadly object with the sharpest of blades. The weapon sparked to life in his free hand and he saw Malak's eyes drawn to it. The killer's armor was impervious to weapons of Heaven, but the flesh inside the shell was not. Aaron plunged the flaming dagger into the chink at the bend of Malak's arm where the armor separated into two pieces.

Malak screeched in pain, sounding more like a wounded animal than anything remotely human, and pulled away his arm, releasing Aaron's throat from his death grip. Aaron scrambled back across the ground, rubbing at is bruised windpipe, greedily taking in gulps f air.

"That hurt," Malak whined, sounding a bit ke the little boy that he should have been. But aron now knew that wasn't the case at all.

With his other arm, the scarlet-garbed war- or raked his hand across an area of open air in ont of him, and tore a hole in space. For the rst time Aaron took note of the sound that it ade, and it reminded him of the ripping of eavy fabric. From his neverending arsenal, the iller produced a loaded crossbow.

The fight was taking its toll. Wearily Aaron ummoned another sword of fire, but his neme- is was faster. As his blade took form, Malak let y a bolt. Aaron lashed out at the shaft of black etal, deflecting the projectile in a shower of parks. With nimble fingers, Malak loaded nother bolt and fired it. This time the Nephilim asn't fast enough and the bolt buried itself eep in the flesh of his thigh.

The pain drove him to his knee. He tried to ull it from his leg, but the shaft was greasy with is own blood. He heard the clatter of armor on e move and saw that Malak was moving ward him, holding a sword as he came in for e kill. Aaron struggled to stand, hefting his wn weapon of fire

It was then that the church exploded. There as a flash from somewhere within the holy ructure, and then it blew apart with a deafening

roar, spewing hungry orange flames into the sky
Glass, metal, and wood rained down upon th
battlefield.

"Master," Malak cried pitifully, his attentio
focused entirely on the blackened, smoking hol
that was Aerie's place of worship.

Malak's show of concern for the monste
that had brought nothing but pain and miser
was all Aaron needed to spur him to action. Thi
was the moment he had both dreaded an
longed for, the opportunity to finally bring th
battle to a close. Time slowed and his le
screeched in protest as he threw himself towar
his distracted enemy. With both hands Aaro
brought the blazing sword up over his shoulde
and then swung it with all the force he coul
muster. As he watched the blade cut through th
air on course to its target, his thoughts wer
filled with images of the past—frozen moment
of time that seemed so very long ago.

He saw the little boy he'd loved sleepin
peacefully in his bed, Gabriel curled into a tigl
ball at his side.

The blade was closer now, and Malak bega
to turn, suddenly aware.

The child rocking before the television se
the image upon the screen nothing more tha
static.

"I'm sorry, Stevie," Aaron whispered as th
heavenly blade reached its destination, cuttin
through the thick muscle and bone of Malak

neck, severing his head from his armored body.

Aaron fell to his knees before the body of his foe—his brother—and bowed his head. He felt drained of life, as if this last, violent act had sucked away his final reserves of strength.

But then he heard something move within the rubble of the church and lifted his head to gaze at the smoldering wreckage. There was a brilliant flash of light, and a warm breeze caressed his face as a figure rose up from beneath the detritus, carried into the air on wings composed of heavenly light.

"Murderer," Verchiel pronounced, his accusation rumbling through the air.

chapter fifteen

No matter how hard she tried, Lorelei could not keep the man from dying.

The attack by the Powers was unrelenting, brutal, and she watched stunned as people who she had come to know as friends were slain before her eyes. Lorelei did what she could, using angelic magicks to repel the attackers, but it wasn't enough. Citizens were still dying.

She did not know him well, but thought his name was Mike. He too was a Nephilim, and had come to Aerie not long after she'd first arrived. He'd had the look—pale skin, close-cropped hair, an unusual amount of scar tissue around the wrists. Like her, he had been institutionalized as the angelic birthright came to life inside him, turning his day-to-day existence on its ear.

Lorelei had seen him struck down. A Powers

angel had come swooping down out of the sky and impaled him on the end of a flaming spear before moving on to find murder and mayhem elsewhere. There was a flash of recognition in his eyes as she approached him, a glimmer of hope that this was not the end for him despite the gaping wound in his chest. If only she had the power. Using all her strength, she dragged him from the street, away from the battle that would decide their fate. On a front lawn more dirt than grass, she knelt down beside him and took his hand in hers.

In the past she'd tried to make small talk with Mike. Whenever she saw him out walking or at the group meetings, she always made it a point to smile and say hello. But Mike had kept to himself. She'd heard that he wasn't adjusting well to his transformation. Right now, it didn't really matter. Mike was dying and there was nothing she could do to save him. All she could do was be with him when he passed.

We're not doing very well, she thought as she gave Mike's hand a gentle squeeze. The dying Nephilim squeezed back weakly. His wound was still smoking, as if burning somewhere deep within, and she placed her other hand over the hole in his chest hoping to smother it.

Her father's guns boomed somewhere in the distance, and she was certain that another Powers' angel had met its fate, but it wasn't enough. Most of the citizens weren't soldiers, and the Powers had sworn their existences to wiping Aerie's kind from the world. Lorelei could sense her fellow Nephilim dying, like tiny pieces of herself floating away on the wind.

She returned her attention to Mike and saw that he had passed away. His eyes were wide in death, staring up into the sky toward what she hoped was a better place, a place where he could be at peace. And wasn't that what they were all fighting for?

She rose and moved to return to the battle. The ground was littered with the corpses of citizens and Powers alike. A Powers' soldier, one of his wings twisted and bent, came at her from across the street. There was a dagger of flame in one hand and the look of murder in his glistening black eyes. She must have looked like an easy target.

"Hate to disappoint you," she said before beginning to mutter a spell of defense. She felt the charge of angelic energy building inside her. The angel was almost upon her, but she held her ground. She could smell the stink of his fury oozing from his flesh; it smelled of spice and something akin to burning rubber. It made her want to vomit.

Lorelei was getting tired. Her body was not used to manipulating these kinds of energies for this length of time, and the magicks were slow to respond. The strain was painful as she called forth a blast of crackling energy. Bolts of energy emanated from her fingertips and met in the air to form a ball. The energy rolled across the space between them, striking the Powers' angel in the face, stopping him in his tracks. The angel screamed pitifully as the flesh on his face turned to ash. He fell to his knees, dead before his body even touched the ground.

Her head swam and the tips of her fingers ached as if frostbitten. She wondered if she'd be able to find the strength to defend herself again, when she felt an uncomfortable tingling in the pit of her stomach and looked past the battles to the church of Aerie. It was Belphegor she sensed, and he was in great pain. But as Lorelei started for the holy place, it exploded in a blast of orange flame and a scorching wind that picked her up and tossed her back. She struggled to her feet and wound her way across the battlefield to the smoking pile of rubble. Not even the destruction of the church could stop their battle.

"Belphegor!" she cried, the heat of the ruins on which she walked burning through the soles of her boots.

It was then that she felt him, a twinge of his once powerful life force calling from nearby. A hand, charred and blackened, beckoned to her from beneath a section of collapsed wall and she went to it. Using all her strength, Lorelei moved the rubble aside, managing to expose Belphegor's upper body. He was hurt beyond imagining, and she hadn't the slightest idea how he was still living.

His breathing was a grating rasp, and his eyes—his beautiful, soulful eyes—opened as she laid her hand upon his blackened cheek.

"Belphegor," she whispered, scalding tears of sadness raining down from her eyes. "What have they done to you?"

The fallen angel closed his eyes again, as if attempting to muster the strength to speak. "I have lost my battle," he said in a strained whisper, his voice like the rustling of dry leaves. "But the war is far from over."

"They're killing us," she said, bowing her head, feeling the grip of despair upon her.

His charred hand brushed against the side of her head, and she raised her gaze to him. "As long as *he* still lives," the Founder stressed, "there is hope."

She wanted to believe in the savior, in Aaron Corbet, but at the moment it all seemed so unrealistic. Instead Lorelei began to move away more of the debris. "Let's see about getting you free—"

"Stop," he commanded, his voice stronger. "It is too late for me," he said with finality.

She didn't want to hear that, she didn't want to hear that he had given up. If he had managed to survive thus far, maybe there was something she could do to help him heal faster. Her thoughts raced with spells of healing. "You can't die." She continued to frantically try to free him. "You have to hold on . . . you have to hold on until the savior forgives you."